"One of the most interesting writers of
  the paperback originals."
—Marv Lachman, *20th Century
  Crime & Mystery Writers*

"If you like your mysteries rough,
  this one is for you."
—*Pittsburgh Press*

"Mr. Lacy offers a solid and original
  story, a brilliantly intricate crime and
  an abundance of wry humor."
—*Washington News*

"It is a vivid, hard-hitting police story—
  with no punches pulled."
—Will Oursler

"Well constructed and harshly
  realistic…"
—*San Francisco Chronicle*

'Tough and fast moving."
—*Cincinnati Enquirer*

D1559022

The Men From the Boys
the Boys
ED LACY

Black Gat Books • Eureka California

THE MEN FROM THE BOYS

Published by Black Gat Books
A division of Stark House Press
1315 H Street
Eureka, CA 95501, USA
griffinskye3@sbcglobal.net
www.starkhousepress.com

THE MEN FROM THE BOYS
Originally published by Harper & Brothers, New
York, copyright © 1956 by Ed Lacy. Reprinted in
paperback by Pocket Books, Inc., New York, 1957.

ISBN-13: 978-1-944520-46-5

Book design by Mark Shepard, SHEPGRAPHICS.COM
Proofreading by Bill Kelly

First Stark House Press Edition: February 2018

FIRST EDITION

ED LACY

be one of
hen your
ground
ed up

ew

jump who
the duty watches

novel must be about people, but not nec-
arily about any particular person or persons. All
names and incidents in this book are imaginary and
not based upon any actual persons, living or dead.

E. L.

One

As if I wasn't feeling bad enough it had t[...]
those muggy New York City summer nights [...]
breath comes out melting. With my room on the [...]
floor and facing nothing, I lay in bed and swea[...]
the joint.

The summer hadn't been too rough till the last [...]
days, about the time my belly went on the rocks, whe[...]
it became a Turkish bath. I stared up at the flaky ceiling
and wished the 52 Grover Street Corporation would in-
stall air conditioning. *Almost* wished I was the house
dick at a better hotel. No, I didn't wish that—I had a
sweet deal at the Grover. With my police pension, the
pocket money the hotel insisted was a salary, and my
various side rackets, I was pulling down over two hundred dollars a week in this flea bag—all of it tax free.

Turning over to reach a cool part of the sheet, this
warm, queasy feeling bubbled through my gut. I belched
and snapping on the table light took a mint. All I had
on was shorts, but they were damp and as I started to
change them, there was a knock on the door.

When I said, "Yeah?" Barbara opened the door, fanning her face with a folded morning paper. She never
slopped around in a kimono or just a slip. Barbara was
always neat in a dress and underthings, and shoes, not
slippers. Which was one reason I let her work the hotel
steadily. Her simple face might have been cute—ten
years ago. Now it held that washed-out look that comes
with the wear and tear. But her legs were still cute, long
and slim.

She closed the door and leaned against it. "My—what
a lump of man."

"You should have seen me when I was younger and real hard—I looked like a tub then, too. What time is it?"

"Eleven-something. I'm knocking off, Marty. Ain't no customers. Guy'd have to be a sex maniac in all this heat."

"All right, take off."

She gave me a tired smile. "Dropped by to see if you wanted anything, maniac."

"Beat it, you sweatbox."

"You ain't kidding, I feel soggy. —Just me and Dora. Jean never showed. I left the money with Dewey."

Another thing I liked about Barbara: she was honest. I got half of every three bucks the girls made. Out of that twenty-five cents went to Dewey, the night clerk, and he took care of Lawson, the bright joker who handled the desk during the day. Kenny, the bellhop, took another fifteen cents besides his tips. Out of my share I handled the pay-off to the cops. The 52 Grover Street Corporation got theirs in the usual way; there was a $2.50 room charge every time. It wasn't big time nor was it exactly penny ante. On a busy week end we often had ten girls working the hotel.

I got into a clean pair of shorts as she asked, "Hitting the sheets so early?"

"My stomach's been a brute. Gas, the runs, and feeling crummy in general."

"Watch what you eat in this heat, Marty. Try some warm milk with a little rice; that will settle your belly. And lay off the bottle."

"Honey, I can't even smoke, much less hold any booze down," I said as the house phone rang.

"Wish my Harold couldn't hold it down. I'm in no mood for any rough stuff."

"Tell your Harold if he puts a hand on you I'll knock

his head from under his fat ears," I said. That was a lie. I wouldn't mind working Harold over, I never had no use for pimps, but the 52 Grover Street Corporation wouldn't like the idea.

All I ever saw of the "Corporation" was Mr. King, an old and busy accountant who came around every day with his skinny nose up in the air. He was both auditor and hotel manager. Actually the Grover was owned by one of the largest and most respectable real-estate outfits in town. Which figured: "respectable" people always owned "houses."

The phone rang again. As I picked it up, Barbara thumbed her nose at me, opened the door. "See you to-morrow, lover."

"All right, honey." Then I asked the phone, "What's the trouble, Dewey?"

"Couple of truckers in 703 hitting a bottle and making noise."

"All right." I hung up and started to dress. Never failed. When I wanted sleep some joker's whiskey had to start talking. Not that the Grover was very rough. Around 1900, I'm told, when this section was full of private houses, it had been a first-rate hotel with a view of the Hudson. Then it became an artists' hangout and speakeasy. When the midtown markets expanded, the Grover was just near enough to get a lot of truckers, along with a few seedy permanents—civil-service work-ers—and some transients who wandered in because they didn't know any better, maybe saw our roof sign from the highway.

Bending down to lace my shoes I brought up some gas and it was like an old sewer coming to life. I needed to see a doctor. The phone rang again. I grabbed it, told Dewey, "All right, I'm going up there!"

"Marty," Dewey's soft voice said, "there's a cop in the

lobby to see you."

"Which one?" The greedy punks knew I paid off direct.

"New one. Sort of looks like a store cop to me. Youngster I never seen before. He asked for you."

"Is he a cop or a uniformed guard?"

"Well," Dewey hesitated, "he looks like a cop and then again he don't. You know, one of them Civil Defense cops, I think."

"All right, tell him to wait. I'll see him in my office and straighten the bastard out."

"Sure, Marty."

I hung up and cursed. Things must be getting bad when a phony cop had nerve enough to be on the take. Hold his hand out to me and I'd break it off.

We had a small self-service elevator in the rear that the maids used during the day and I took it up to the seventh floor. These two clowns in 703 were singing and as I passed 715, Mr. Ross, one of the permanents, an old crotchety baldheaded bookkeeper, was waiting by his open door. He said, "Really, Mr. Bond, on a warm weekday night, this is an outrage!"

"They'll quiet down in a minute, Mr. Ross. Go back to sleep."

"Sleep? In this heat?"

"The Grover isn't responsible for the weather," I said, a poor joke that Ross didn't crack a smile over. Of course I could tell him a few things Barbara had told me about him that would make Ross hysterical, but I kept on walking down the hallway.

I knocked three times on 703, but the two of them were harmonizing on some hillbilly ditty and didn't hear me. They sure couldn't sing a little. I had my coat on and a tie, and my shirt was damp already. Opening the door with a passkey, I stepped inside and shut it quickly. I'd never seen these truck jockeys before. They were both about twenty-seven, tall and lean, cocky punks. They were lying on their beds, each working on a pint, and wearing dungarees and shoes. There was an empty fifth on the floor. They jumped to their feet when they saw me. They were nicely built boys, ridges of muscles across their stomachs. The smaller one asked, "Don't you ever knock?"

"I knocked—you were blowing your nose too loud to hear me."

The bigger one said, "Don't have to ask who you are—house dick written all over your fat puss."

"That's me. Look, it's hot, I don't want no trouble. How about sleeping it off?"

"Want a shot?" the smaller trucker asked, waving his bottle at me.

"Too hot. I just want what you guys need—some sleep," I said. This bitter-greasy taste suddenly flooded my mouth as the big one winked at his buddy. I got sore. On a steaming night these clowns wanted trouble, a little action. I got a mint in my mouth and chewed it quickly.

Big boy said, "We feel like singing. We're happy. Got us a load going back just like that." He tried to snap his fingers.

"You want to sing, go down on the docks and sing your fool heads off." I nodded at the beds. "Also, you ain't on the farm now and this ain't no pigpen—take your shoes off when you hit the sack."

The smaller guy came toward me, waving his bottle. "Aw, have a drink with me."

I wanted them both in close—although they didn't look like bottle throwers. I made one last effort. I said, "It's awful hot, no point in any of us working up a sweat. Take off your shoes and cut the singing! Tomorrow I'll take that drink."

"Kind of old and fat for all that tough talk, ain't you, baldy?" the big one asked.

"All you whiskey-big-mouthed jokers give me a headache," I said as I hooked the smaller one in the gut. He landed on the bed, skidded off onto the floor, fighting for breath and puking all over the old plush carpet. Big boy didn't move fast at all. I grabbed his bottle hand, jerked him to me and kicked his shin. He sat down hard, holding the leg, rye spilling over one bed.

"It's very hot, let's not have no more exercise," I said.

"You fat bastard, I'll kill you!"

I pulled big boy up by his hair, planted a solid one under his ribs and let him sprawl on the floor. His hands clutched at his belly, clawing at the skin.

That was it: they'd never been hit like that before and their eyes were all fear. I said, "Either of you have any ideas about pulling a knife, forget it. I can give you a real beating if you're asking for it. I asked you in a nice way, but you hardheads got to get smacked down." I glanced around the dirty room. If they had a return trip set, they were loaded. "You slobs made a mess of this room, ruined the rug. Be trouble if the chambermaid yells. Maybe hotel sues you. Best you leave her a tip—now."

The smaller guy rolled over and dug into his pocket.

"Be ten bucks to clean the rug, at least. And worth another ten for the work she'll have to do," I added.

He waved a fistful of bills at me. Nothing like a wallop in the gut to take the starch out of a rough stud. I reached over—carefully—picked up two tens. As I opened the door I told them, "Now go to bed or poppa will have to spank again."

"We'll never come here again!" big boy gasped.

"You do, I'll throw you out the front door. Go to a flop joint where you belong." I shut and locked the door, waited in the hallway for a moment. The clowns weren't marked—if they yelled they couldn't prove a thing. They were stupid drunk and fighting when I came in.

I was sweating a lot and stopped in at my bathroom, washed up, and it was a lucky move, for I got a sudden cramp. When I was ready I took a mint and called Dewey. "Room 703 is okay. Now send that jerky cop into my office."

In my office I took out my wallet and left it open on the desk so my card in the Policeman's Benevolent Association showed—to let the punk know who he was talking to.

He was a young cop, slight, with a skinny chicken neck, and the face looked a little familiar. He sure looked like a real cop, except for the patch on his shoulder, and the badge was smaller and the cap looked cheap. He had a gun belt on with bullets but no gun. Just a night stick and something in his back pocket that could be a sap.

He stood in the doorway, a silly grin on his narrow face, held out his arms like he was modeling the stingy uniform; asked, "Like it, Marty?"

For a moment I didn't recognize him. Hell, the last time I'd seen the kid was during the war, and he wasn't more than a dozen years old then. The grin on his face faded as he asked, "Marty, don't you remember me?"

The sort of plea in his voice did it. I jumped up and shook his small hand. "Lawrence, boy! Where do you come off with that not-remembering line? I was merely dazzled by the blue. Come on, put it down. When did you get the badge?" He always was a frail kid and now he looked compact, but like a weak welterweight. On his collar he had a gold A.P.—auxiliary police.

He sat down opposite me, pleased with himself. "Well,

I'm not exactly a real cop. I'm with Civil Defense and we put in a few hours a week doing patrol duty—sort of practice for us, in case there ever should be an emergency, a bombing and all that. But I'm going to take the police physical next fall. I've been building myself up for it, go to the college gym every day."

"How's your mother?" The kid had always been muscle-happy and cop-crazy. Maybe because he was always so delicate and sickly.

"Just fine. Guess you know she married again?"

"Yeah, I heard. Right after the war, and to some duck working in the aircraft factory with her. Hope she's happy. I gave Dot a rough time."

"Mom never understood you," Lawrence said. He had a good voice, deep and relaxed, and when you looked at his eyes for a while, you knew he was no longer a kid but a man. "Marty, I didn't mean to barge in on you so late, but I was just assigned to this precinct, and ... uh ... I thought you'd still be up."

"I never hit the sack before three or four in the morning. Lately I've had some bum food and my stomach won't let me sleep anyway. You say you're going to college?"

He nodded. "Law school. I wanted to work and go nights, but Dot has been simply wonderful—insisted upon putting me through day school."

"What's the idea of this tin-badge deal?"

He flushed. "Actually, I thought it would help me, give me a working idea of the force, so when I pass the physical and become a real ..."

"You're studying to be a shyster—why you want to be a cop?"

He smiled as if I'd said something clever. "With the name Bond, what else could I be? Some of the men at the station, the regular police, asked me if I was related to you."

"Down in this precinct—they remember me?"

"Every cop remembers you."

"Are you ... uh ... defense cops under the precinct captain?"

"No, we have our own setup. Before this I was assigned to a station house up in the Bronx. But I mingle with the real cops."

"They giving you a hard time because of me?"

He opened his collar, pushed his cap back, said flatly, "No one gives me a hard time, not the son of Marty Bond, the toughest cop on the force." He sounded pretty hard. The kid could be more rugged than he looked—or nuts.

"That what they still call me?"

He turned his palms up, waved them. "Oh, a few said something about the ... uh ... Graham case, that you gave the force a black eye. But I told them off, reminded them you were the most cited man in the history of the New York City police force."

"Graham—that lousy black bastard!"

"How's the hotel business?"

"Dull. Forget being a cop, Lawrence. It's a no-good job, everybody hates your heart."

"I wouldn't say that. Laws are vital, living things to me that need protection, proper enforcement." He lowered his voice. "After all, I not only have your name but my father died in harness. I belong on the force. And if I can only put on a little more muscle, I'll make a good cop."

I was about to tell him there wasn't any such animal as a "good" cop, there couldn't be, but it was too warm to argue. So I said, "Hear there's a lot of college boys on the force."

He grinned again and if it wasn't for his skinny neck

he'd look okay. "Who isn't a college grad these days with the G.I. Bill? Did you know I put in two years in the army?"

"Get overseas?"

"No such luck, I never even got out of Fort Dix." He looked around my office which seemed even crummier in the nighttime. "All this—hotel business—must be rather tame for you, isn't it, Marty?"

"Bounce a drunk now and then, catch a character running out with all his clothes on. That's about it."

"Ever try your own agency?"

"That's strictly movie stuff." There was a moment of silence till I kicked the drawer of my desk, asked, "Want a shot?"

"No, thanks. Are you still married to that dancer, Marty?"

"She wasn't much of a dancer. No, we busted up after a year or so. You married?"

"Not yet, but I will be soon as I get on the force." His eyes studied my face. "Somehow you look ... lonely ... Dad."

"Been a lot of years since you called me that." The silly kid was always calling me Dad or Daddy.

"I always liked calling you Dad. Made me feel proud."

"Yeah? So you think I'm lonely. I work and I sleep and the days go by. Except for this bad food I must have eaten last week, I get along okay. Suppose you've met Lieutenant Ash at the station house?"

"Indeed I did. Funny, I didn't recall ever seeing him, but he stopped me, asked if I wasn't Lawrence Bond, knew all about me. He looks like a square shooter, competent. How long were you partners?"

"Never added it up—maybe fifteen years. We were a good team. Used to say I was the brawn and he was the brains. Yeah, Bill Ash knows his business ... I guess."

There was another silence and the more I stared at the kid the more he looked like his father, except the senior Lawrence had been beefy. I never knew him—he'd walked into a stick-up and with a gun in his back had gone for his own revolver. I was pounding a beat then, and when the boys passed the hat for the widow, I was elected to bring the money to her. I often thought of Dot, the four years our marriage held up. She was a sweet girl, a real homebody. And Lawrence had been a quiet stringbean who thought I was the greatest thing ever.

I must have been daydreaming for quite a time, for suddenly he said, "Look, Marty, I've wanted to see you for a long time. But it was only when I talked to Lieutenant Ash that I even knew where you were. However I've also come to you for advice. A queer ... uh ... incident happened on my post a couple of hours ago and nobody at the precinct house is interested."

I laughed. "I know how it is, your first collar always seems the greatest crime.... Wait a minute, can you volunteer cops make an arrest?"

"Yes, while we're on duty. Technically we're peace officers while in uniform. It's true this is the first ... case ... or trouble I've had, but I don't think that's a factor," Lawrence said seriously.

I could hardly keep from smiling. Maybe he was twenty-one or twenty-two, but he still acted like a kid with a box-top badge. "What was the arrest?"

"There wasn't any arrest. You see, we do patrol duty in pairs and I was walking along Barron Street with my partner, an older man named John Breet. Well, the truth is he stopped at a bar to see if he could get a drink on the cuff. I don't go for that nonsense so I was standing outside the bar. A few doors down there's a small wholesale butcher, the Lande Meat Company. Not much, a double store with the windows painted black. The fact is, Wilhelm Lande, the owner, has had the place closed for the past several weeks. Willie, that's what they call Mr. Lande, says he had a stroke and his doctor advised him to take it easy. He's rather a nervous type."

"What did he want you to do, steady his hand?" I cornballed, thinking how batty a joker has to be to do police work for free.

"Marty, this isn't any joking matter. I have a feeling there's something seriously wrong here."

"All right, you haven't even told me what the beef is."

"Well, you see, they have to give us night tours, but they try to keep them during the light hours as much as possible. It was a little after 7 P.M. when a kid ran up and told me somebody had just broken the window of the butcher shop—from the inside. I didn't wait for Breet. I ran over to the shop and the door wasn't locked, and inside there's Lande the butcher tied up. He'd been robbed and trussed up around 6 P.M. according to his first statement, had finally managed to get ahold of a stapling machine, threw it at the window. I should say he was hysterical, almost in a state of shock as I untied him. He yelled he had been robbed of fifty thousand dollars by two teen-age kids."

"Fifty grand? He must have a big insurance cover," I said.

"That's one aspect of the case that has a false ring," Lawrence said. "While I was taking down the details, and he gave me a fairly clear description of the kids, he suddenly shut up. Might call it abrupt, the way he did it. Said he had to make a phone call. Now, he has a little office in the store and a desk outside the office with a phone, and he dialed a number, whispered something about the holdup. I think I heard him say, 'I'm not sure, they knocked me out.' I wouldn't swear to that, but I

thought he said that. The point is, he must have mentioned that a cop was there—you see, he thought I was
a real policeman—for I saw him glance at me and nod
as he said 'Yes, yes.' He listened for a couple of minutes,
then hung up. When he came back to me, Lande was a
new man, very calm, all one big smile. This will amaze
you, he did a complete about-face in his story! He said
the robbery had been something he dreamed, went to
his icebox and brought out a canned ham, offered it to
me, telling me there never was any fifty thousand, nor
any two holdup men. Told me to forget the whole thing."

I asked, "Where's the ham?"

"Marty, the man was trying to bribe me!"

"All right, all right, so you passed up a ham. How did
he explain his being tied up?"

Lawrence pulled out a pack of butts, offered me one.
I hadn't been able to smoke a cigarette all week, made
me gag. I shook my head and as he lit one, sent a cloud
of smoke out of his nose, the kid said, "That's the very
first thing I asked about. He couldn't think very fast,
gave me some clumsy cock-and-bull story about he'd
seen an actor in a movie tie himself up, and he was
trying it when he had an attack, felt he was choking,
had thrown the stapling machine at the window to get
help. He kept changing his story after the phone call. I
wanted him to come to the station house with me, but
he kept telling me to forget it, not to make a report.
That's it. Like to see my on-the-spot notes?"

"No. What's the beef? He claims there wasn't any
holdup."

"But ..."

"Lawrence, far as you're concerned it's over. Don't go
looking for work, even when you're playing at being a
cop."

The kid flushed. "I don't consider this exactly *play-*

ing—while I'm on duty I am a peace officer with certain powers."

"All I meant was, don't stick your neck out unless you have to."

"Wait till you hear the rest of it, Marty. I was in there about three-quarters of an hour. When I came out Breet wasn't in sight. I phoned the station house and the sergeant—*our* sergeant—bawled me out. Said Breet had returned and what the hell was I doing on patrol alone, all that. Our sergeant is a bit of a pompous old jerk, had me return to the precinct, wouldn't pay any attention to my story. So I went over his head, told Lieutenant Ash— he told me to forget it, too."

"But of course you didn't?" I almost felt sorry for the kid, he was so badge-happy it was comical.

"No, I didn't. Truth is when we were dismissed I went back there—about an hour ago—and Lande was still in his shop. As I told you, he's nervous, talks a blue streak. Well, he made a slip. In his chatter he said, 'I got the money back.' I distinctly heard him say that although he denied it when I questioned him. He made a joke of it, asked where in the devil would he get fifty grand. As it happens, when I was returning to the station house I made a few casual inquiries in the neighborhood, at a bar and at a restaurant—Lande has been selling meat there for the last seven or eight years, does his own butchering, but has a small panel delivery truck and employs a driver. Everybody agrees he was lucky to clear five thousand dollars a year and ..."

"Lawrence, you told him you were an auxiliary cop, didn't you?"

The kid nodded. "He noticed my shoulder patch when I returned, practically ordered me out of the store. I explained that ..."

"You use your stick on him?"

Lawrence looked astonished. "Hit him? Certainly not."

"Then he can't make any complaints, so what's troubling you? And even if you got bounced off this volunteer force, so what?"

"I don't have a 'so what' attitude. I plan to make the force my career and therefore ..."

"You talk like a bad cops-and-robbers movie, like a jerk."

The kid went white and stood up. "Marty, you were a great cop, a top detective. I bring you a case, a crime, and all you can say is ..."

"Sit down, Lawrence," I said, trying to make my voice soft. I slipped him a grin. "It's a hot night and we haven't seen each other for a lot of years. All right, maybe this is important to you, but as for me—one thing I learned while I was a kid—never work for free." He sort of slumped in his chair and I added, "Seems to me you're making a fuss over nothing—the butcher isn't making any charges. And he could even jam you up—when you went back there you weren't on duty, had no police powers—not even as a peace officer, whatever that is."

"I know that," Lawrence said. "But if you could only have seen how hysterical he was at first—I believe he was robbed of fifty thousand dollars and that for some reason the money was returned to him."

"Aren't you getting a little ... uh ... hysterical, kid? You said yourself he doesn't do a business to have that kind of cash around, and if he was robbed, why would it be returned to him? And in a few hours' time, too? It doesn't make sense. Far as you're concerned, forget it."

The kid stared at me for a second, his eyes thoughtful. "Marty, I'm certain there *was* a robbery."

"So what? You're not involved."

"Not involved? It happened on my beat, and if for no other reason I'm involved because as a citizen it's my duty to report any crime I ..."

"You really believe this slop you're handing me?"

"I certainly do!"

"You better forget trying to become a cop, then. Kid, I'm going to give you some advice I'm sure you won't pay no attention to, but just in case you do become a cop, or even this part-time stuff you're doing, I don't want to see you make a fool of yourself. There's hardly ..."

"I fail to understand your attitude toward the law, Marty!"

"Relax, and listen to me. There's hardly a day goes by in which the average citizen doesn't break some law—maybe letting his dog off a leash or spitting on the sidewalk. Also, there's hundreds of laws, maybe thousands, that don't make sense and shouldn't be on the books. For example, a girl can be hustling ever since she's thirteen, selling it a dozen times a day, yet until she's eighteen every one of her customers is guilty of statutory rape. Isn't that something, raping a whore!"

"A prostitute has rights, the protection of the law. The very fact that she may be under age proves ..."

"Damn it, Lawrence, stop talking like a schoolboy reciting his lessons," I said. "You dream of being a cop, then remember this—a cop only enforces the laws he *has* to, otherwise he'd go nuts—looks the other way whenever he can. Maybe this ..."

"That's not my idea of law enforcement. At all times the ..."

"Shut up! Maybe your butcher was robbed, maybe he wasn't. He says he wasn't. Maybe he also exceeded the speed limit driving to his shop today. Lawrence, what I'm trying to say is, don't be an eager beaver. Here you're only a volunteer cop for a couple hours a week, and you're already in an uproar over something that's none of your business. And don't hand me that honest-citizen crap. Lande's story is so wacky it can be true. He's robbed of fifty grand he says he hasn't, then an hour later the punks return the dough all tied in pink ribbons—probably said they were bad boys. Forget it."

"I can't, there's too many weird angles. If only for curiosity's sake, I'm going to keep looking into this."

"The cemeteries are full of curious people."

"Marty, you've slowed down."

"Maybe. And maybe if you were a stranger I'd knock you through the wall, badge, club, and all. Maybe that's what Lande should have done. Lawrence, I can't tell you what to do, but don't make a horse's rear out of yourself, especially if you might get on the force someday."

"Marty, I'm not a kid looking for a thrill. I think there's something wrong here. I have a feeling, a hunch— and Lande's cockeyed story."

I shrugged, dug for another mint. I was all out of the damn things. "Told you—you wouldn't take my advice. Do what you want, only try not to make a fool of yourself."

He got to his feet. "Anyway, it's good to see you. I'll drop in to see you again, if you don't mind."

I stood up and squeezed his shoulder. He didn't have much meat on him. "Where do you get that if-you-don't-mind slop? Drop in any time. Maybe we'll have supper together when my gut is hitting on all cylinders. You see Dot much?"

"Of course. I'm living at home."

"Tell her I asked for her. Ain't you kind of old for still living at home? What's the name of your girl and are you sleeping with her?"

"That's none of your business, but we have been intimate. Name is Helen Samuels."

"Sounds like a Jew."

"She is. Why are you so bigoted, Marty?"

"You really going to marry a Jew-girl?"

"Why not?"

I shrugged. "I'm hardly the one to give advice on marriage. Also I'm not bigoted. I've known some pretty good nigger cops and Jew-boys. And Bill Ash is a Roman. I don't know, as a cop you got to start off by hating a lot of people, most people. Makes it easier to hate 'em if you hate their skin, their religion."

He sort of laughed at me, punched my arm. It was odd, all of him was a kid except his eyes and his voice. He said, "You're like a rock, Marty, unchangeable. Remember when you gave me boxing lessons? I was a fair bantamweight in the army."

We walked toward the door. "If I'd known you were going to be such a busybody, I would have given you lessons in kneeing and kicking."

I walked the kid out to the lobby and said good-by. It was a few minutes past midnight on the clock behind the desk when I grabbed a morning paper, told Dewey, "Maybe I can get some shut-eye now."

Dewey was a retired postal clerk, a moonface with watery eyes, and the veins on his fat nose like a complicated map—from the barrels of wine he'd guzzled during his sixty-eight years.

He said, "Too hot for sleep. The boy badge have his hand out?"

"No—merely dropped in to see me."

"Funny-looking cop. He's too young to have been on the force with you."

"He was my son—for a few years," I said, walking toward my room. Dewey never even blinked.

I washed my teeth and took a shower, felt pretty good. Then I stretched out on my bed and read the paper, starting backward from the sporting page.

There wasn't a damn thing in the paper: the Giants' shortstop turned his ankle, the Dodgers still had a "mathematical" chance of getting the pennant, and the comics weren't funny. There was a cheesecake picture of some lush babe asking for a divorce because her marriage was "kissless." A mild-looking guy named Mudd was accused of taking a bank for forty-five thousand dollars with a toy gun, and Albert Bochio, the syndicate treasurer, was still barricaded in a Miami hotel daring the authorities to boot him out, talking out of both sides of his mouth about suing the city of Miami for calling him a "gangster." And the front page had the usual war scare.

One of the columnists hinted that the fight game was crooked, and also commented on the fact Bochio was never so headline-brave before. There was a standard item about a Hollywood busted marriage "which will spill dirt all over the papers when it comes to court."

I tossed the paper on the floor and turned off the light. Somehow the promised dirt never came out and I wondered if the columnists ran these items when they were short of material. And a guy has to have more courage than people think to use a toy gun in a stick-up. But they were right about Bochio—one of those unknown big shots. He was rapped once for assault when he was twenty-three, then dropped out of the gang picture till a Senate television show spotlighted him as the pillar of a swank New Jersey community, son at Yale, daughter in some finishing school ... and holder of the purse strings of the biggest crime mob in the country.

I turned over a couple of times, got comfortable. Wondered how soon Lawrence would find out about me and the hotel. As a part-time cop he wouldn't know the score. And what did I care if he did?

It turned a bit cool and I covered myself with the sheet and dropped off. I awoke just before six, sweating like a pig, the dream still with me. Crazy, I hadn't had *that* dream in years ... this Mrs. DeCosta's face screwed up with hate, screaming at me, "*You thug with a badge!*" I could see her plainly, as if she was next to me—and that wouldn't have been bad either, she was a fine-looking chick. What the hell she want to marry that crippled spick artist for?

Probably dreamed of her because I'd been thinking of Dot. Women ... Now, why did Dot have to leave me because of that? The beatings were none of her business. And what finally became of the DeCosta blonde, or was she still in the loony bin?

I stretched and sat up, the stink still in my mouth. I was all done with sleep so I turned on the radio and then I got to thinking about Mudd who'd taken the bank with a toy rod. How did they know his name? Turning on the light I picked up the paper, read the whole piece this time. Amateur crooks are dumb as hell.... Mudd had been a depositor in the very bank he held up. By this time the cops would have him for sure.

I got up and showered. Except for my breath I felt pretty good. Not eating or drinking much, being on the run this last week, along with the heat, had taken about ten pounds off me. My muscles were showing again.

Dressing in a tropical blue suit that proved "bargains" aren't for big men, I walked through the lobby. One of the maids was starting to clean up, still half asleep, and Dewey was pounding his ear in the big chair behind the desk—his favorite bed. As I went through the doorway, Lawson the day clerk (and elevator pilot and bellhop) was coming in. He was sporting a silk polo shirt and a crew cut, a big book under his arm. He was always reading, and was probably a fag—went around with the Village artists. He glanced at the way my suit hung on me, asked, "A circus come with that tent?"

"Why? You want a job as a fire-eater? Probably the only thing you don't eat."

"Your humor is like your suit—it doesn't fit you. Up early, aren't you, Mr. Bond?"

"Yeah, I'm checking on your time."

His thin lips gave me what passed for a sneer. "They got a nerve, with the twelve-hour day I put in."

"You going for a union here?" Wouldn't surprise me if the smart bastard was a radical. We all put in long hours, but the gravy was worth it. And Lawson didn't do a damn thing but read. We never got busy till late afternoon and Dewey was on then.

I walked over to Hamilton Square and had coffee and toast, got hungry and knocked off a stack of pancakes, a hunk of pie, and more coffee. It was only seven and I had nothing to do.

Walking over to Washington Park, I sat around for a while watching some old nut open a bag of crumbs and feed the pigeons. When a couple of them hopped up on his hands, he glanced at me proudly. I decided to take a bus ride uptown, buy some socks and a couple of shirts. I rode up to Fifty-seventh Street and then down to Macy's, but the store wasn't open yet. I had a glass of iced coffee and tried smoking a cigarette.

A lot of gas hit my stomach and I began belching, so I took an Alka-Seltzer and bought a pack of mints. The pain in my gut hit me and I forgot about shopping.

I phoned Art Dupre's office and got one of these answering services. I found his home phone in the Bronx book. He answered with "Dr. Dupre speaking."

"Doctor, I'm in trouble," I said in a gal's voice.

"Who is this?"

"Oh, doctor, I'm in trouble and I ain't married and

the druggist said you'd fix it for me."

"Who is this? What doctor do you want?"

"Oh, you a doctor? I want Sergeant Dupre!" I said in my regular voice.

Art said, "Marty Bond—you and your lousy gags. How are you?"

"Got a touch of ptomaine poisoning, or something, Art. My belly is acting up. Can you work on me sometime this morning?"

"Of course. How about eleven?"

"All right."

"How sick are you, Marty? Vomiting?"

"Naw, but I feel like it at times. Mostly the runs and an upset gut. I'll live till eleven—the question is, Will I live after you work on me?"

"That's a bright question, the enlisted man's dream come true—having his C.O. coming to him for help. See you at eleven, and don't drink anything cold or strong in the meantime."

"Okay, boy."

I still had a couple of hours to kill so I took the bus downtown. The sun was already out strong, another scorcher. I took off my coat and thought about going to Coney Island, or surf casting at Jones Beach. But I was looking forward to seeing Art. He'd been a medic in my M.P. outfit and saved me from a lot of grief over in England when I nearly killed a cocky A.W.O.L. wop.

That kid Art had the stuff, he wanted to be a doc and he'd made it. G.I. Bill was something, except for us older guys. I would have looked silly going to college. And what could I learn—you never needed no bill to go to my college, the University of Hard Knocks.

I got off at Hamilton Square and headed for the precinct. Some white-haired bag was standing on the corner, rattling a red tin can. Pushing it up in my face, she gave me the pitch-smile as she asked, "Please help fight cancer?"

"Let the government shell out the dough for it. They're always spending dough like water."

"We must all chip in and do our part," she said sweetly. She probably worked for a percentage of the take.

"Your sexy smile does it, sister," I said, dropping a couple of dimes in the can.

"Thank you. Like to put this on your coat?" She held up a red tin button shaped like a sword.

"They giving medals for being a sucker now?" I asked, winking at her and walking on.

It was a big morning for me. When I asked the desk man for Lieutenant Ash he said, "The lieutenant isn't in yet. What do you want to see him about?"

He was another of these slim cops, young too—under forty. "Just dropped in for some chatter. When do you expect him?"

"About noon."

"I'll be back. Tell him Marty Bond called."

"I'll tell him." He gave me a mild stare.

"Yeah, Marty Bond the ex-cop," I said, walking out. I dropped in at the Grover and Lawson said, "Mr. King is in the office."

"So what?"

"Just thought you'd like to know. Room 703 checked out leaving the room a mess. The rug will have to be cleaned."

"It's about time."

"Mr. King was miffed about it."

"He miffs too easy." I took the elevator up to the seventh floor. Lilly, one of the old colored chambermaids, was cleaning 703. She said, "Look at this mess. It's disgusting."

"Couple of drunks. I had to quiet them last night. By

the way, Lilly, they left this as a tip for you." I handed her five bucks. "Clean up the room good before King comes sniffing up here."

She pocketed the fin quickly. "I'll take care of it. That was nice of them to think of me."

"I sort of suggested it. Put it all on a number and you can retire—maybe. What do you like for today?"

"I usually stick along with my house number, 506."

"All right, play a buck for me."

"I'll get it in. Where's the money?"

"Lilly, out of the five. Wasn't for me you wouldn't have nothing."

I went down to my room, considered shaving, dabbed some after-shave lotion under my armpits, put on a fresh shirt, and went out. Art had his offices on East Fifty-eighth Street—pretty swank. I took a bus to Fifty-second Street and walked through the ratty section between Sixth and Fifth Avenues that's full of night spots. I knew Flo was stripping in one of the joints and for no reason I wanted to see her picture.

She wasn't the feature strip; they only had an 8" x 10" of Flo, one of her old snaps. I stared at the strong long legs, the hard body, the hard beautiful face, the small, perfect breasts. This snap was taken nine years ago, but Flo hadn't changed much. Whenever she worked one of the burleycue houses in New Jersey, I'd go over to watch her. Almost gave me a queer bang to see the clowns gaping at her, recalling all the times I'd had what they were eyeballing.

Although I never really *had* Flo. I was tough, but she was tougher. She was about the toughest babe I ever knew. She knew what she had, and her only aim in life was to make it pay off in folding dough. I remembered the first time I saw her, in the chorus of a crummy Broadway musical. Guess she went with me for a resting pe-

riod. My salary gave her a chance to hunt around for a
feature role, study up on her dancing and acting. Everything she did was part of this drive to "get to the top."
You couldn't even beat this drive out of her—I tried it a
couple of times.

Maybe one of the reasons I got a kick out of seeing
Flo do her act, these last couple of years, was the satis-
faction in knowing she'd never made the top. She left
me for a bastard who took her out to Hollywood. Flo
had all the whistle stops, enough ability, but she must
have slept with the wrong jokers. Over the years I'd see
her in a few bit parts, then in '48 she started doing burlesque work, night clubs. Flo had to be hitting thirty-
eight or thirty-nine now, just sticking around for the
crumbs.

I walked slowly toward Madison Avenue thinking of
Flo. If only she had had something in her blood besides
ambition we might have hit things off—for a short time
we had it pretty good. I used to wake up in the middle
of the night, light a match and stare at her, wondering
how a slob like me ever got so lucky. Dot had the brains
and the warmth, Flo had the body. Although Dot could
surprise the hell out of you—sometimes.

Art was sharing the first floor of a brownstone with
two other doctors. I gave the nurse at the reception desk
my name and she told me to sit down. I slipped a mint
in my mouth and watched her legs under the desk, wondered why I was looking—Barbara had better stems.
And in any event what good would ...?

I belched and watched her face to see if she'd heard.
She hadn't. I glanced around the office, all the modern
furniture. The last time I had Art work on me was a
year ago. He had a modest office up on Eighty-third
Street then. The boy was climbing fast.

After a couple of minutes Art came in, looking fine in

his white jacket. Although he wasn't a ladies' man, he could be—had one of these lean, homely maps that women go for, like Gary Cooper. And Art was big and fairly muscular although he never did any physical work or exercise. Once in the army when we were swimming in Venice, I asked him how he stayed in shape and he'd said, "I don't know, lieutenant. I suppose I was just born this way." Art never called me "sir," always "lieutenant," which was okay with me.

After the usual hard handshake and cracks about neither of us looking a day older, I followed him into his neat office, sat down in a chair that looked like a giant ice-cream cone and which turned out to be comfortable. "How's the hotel business, Marty?" he asked, taking out my file.

"All right. With the housing shortage, hotels are making out."

He nodded, as though he was interested. "What's all this about ptomaine? Upset stomach? According to my records you're a typical hard rock. An interesting specimen, a throwback, as I kept telling you, a ..."

"All right, cut the big words. So I'm a specimen, pickled alcohol, and all that. Art, I think I have a case of the old G.I.'s. Been that way, off and on—and that's no pun— for the last few weeks. Nothing seems to help. Also, I have a lousy taste in my mouth, like something died in me a long time ago."

"Any fever or chills?"

"Nope, I don't think so. I sweat, but that's because of the dog days we've been having. I belch a lot."

"Still drinking?"

"Nope. Funny thing, haven't had a desire for a shot, or for a cigarette either."

"According to my records you haven't had anything worse than an acid stomach in the last five years. You look like your usual burly gorilla self. Though what's left of your hair is turning gray. Marty, you worrying about anything?"

"Me? I never worried in my life."

He stood up. "I'd say you're in good shape—for an old man."

"I'm only fifty-four, you punk."

"Okay, pops, take off your shirt and I'll give you the works."

The boy really gave me a thorough examination, worked me over with several gadgets, put me in front of a fluoroscope ... all the time asking questions about what I liked to eat and what I didn't, the color and shape of my bowels, any pains, and other exciting remarks.

At first we were wisecracking a lot, but after a while I knew he was putting on an act with the gags—Art was really damn serious, even frightened.

After about an hour he told me to dress and we sat down at his desk. Art asked, "Marty, you say you're always tired, weak, not much of an appetite, lost weight and ..."

"All right, Art, stop stalling, what's wrong with me?"

"Well," he said slowly, "I think you have a tumor, a growth next to your intestines ... far as I can make out. You may need an operation. I'm sending you to a specialist for a gastric X ray. He'll know much more about it than I do."

"I have a tumor in my gut?" I repeated.

"I *think* you have one."

"Can't penicillin, one of these new wonder drugs, do the trick?"

"Perhaps. We'll see what the specialist says. You may not even require surgery. But I think it will be best to take a sample of the growth. Merely routine ..."

"A sample? You mean it might be cancer?" The words seemed to sting as they tumbled out of my lips.

"Might be anything," Art said casually. "Marty, I'm only a pill-and-temperature man, wait till we hear what the big shot says. I can be all wrong about it being a tumor. I'll make an appointment for you."

I sat like a dummy, hearing Art pick up the phone, make an appointment for 1:30 the following afternoon. I couldn't think. All I could do was taste the dry garlic stink on my tongue. There was a horse cop I knew who died of cancer of the gut. He'd been a pro boxer once and we used to work out together. He'd starved to death because the cancer squeezed his intestines tight. I spent a lot of time with him in the hospital, watching him become a bag of bones.

As Art put the phone down I told him, "I was never afraid of dying because if you don't fear death you got the world by the tail. But this ... what a crummy way of going out."

"Stop it. It could be an ulcer, an inflated stomach, a hundred and one things besides ..."

"Don't talk a hole in my head, Art!"

He stared at me for a second, then pulled a pipe out of a drawer, carefully packed and lit it. "Marty, this isn't something you can lick with hard talk or slugging, so don't be a goddam amateur doctor. Every growth isn't cancer, just as every headache isn't a nervous breakdown. If it is a tumor they cut it out and in a few weeks you're good as new. It's that simple."

I shook my head. "It'll be cancer."

"Oh for—How do you know? I ..."

"*Hell, I just know!*"

"You're spouting sheer nonsense. Wait till you hear what the specialist tells you tomorrow before starting the dramatics and self-pity. Not like you, I always thought you were too tough for fear." Art smiled. "That's hot air I'm handing you, Marty. I don't blame you for being frightened, but if I don't know what it is, *you* certainly don't. Let me know what the specialist tells you tomorrow."

"As if he won't call you. Art, if it should be cancer, how much time ...?"

"I refuse to answer that, even think of it."

"I once knew a guy that had it, right in the gut too. Lay in bed for over three months before he finally kicked off, looked like a goddam skeleton."

"Marty, let me give it to you straight. If it is cancer you may die. I said *if* and *may*. Not every cancer patient dies, most of them live. As for dying, you know the old bromide—a car may splatter your brains all over the street the second you leave this office."

"Hell, that's quick."

Art came around the desk, slapped me on the shoulder. "Marty, you make me ashamed of myself for being such a bad doctor, scaring a patient. Wouldn't have told you except I thought you were such a tough bastard. I don't have the knowledge or equipment to diagnose this, so if it turns out to be a gas pocket, something as silly as that, don't try to whip my head. Now, here's the specialist's name and address. Be on time and be ready to shell out about fifty bucks. Need any money?"

I got up. "No. What do I owe you?"

"I enjoyed your company."

I dropped a five spot on his desk. "This do it?"

"I told you ..."

I shoved his hand away. "I've heard that north wind before. So long, Art."

"Marty, let's have supper together. I never see you except when you're sick. How about making it for Friday ...?"

"Sure. I'll call you."

I walked out, passed by the receptionist, and the lousy taste was strong in my mouth. The taste of death, the greasy crummy taste of death. I stood on the sidewalk for a few minutes trying to swallow, clear my mouth. The sun was making me sweat. I didn't know what to do. I wanted to talk to somebody, go home. But home was a flea-bag hotel room.

I had a sudden desire to see Flo, to be with her in the flashy four-room apartment we used to have, the little bar and bar stools like in the movies. There was the bedroom with Flo's dolls....

Dolls made me snap out of it. I had no time for dolls or for much of anything else. I walked to a corner drug-store, bought some mints and drank two glasses of or-angeade that I damn near threw up.

I took a cab down to Hamilton Square. Bill Ash had been my boon buddy for a lot of years. He was a good listener, a guy with a level brain. I crossed the Square and headed toward the station house. Bill and I had been attached to a precinct uptown for almost six years before we were sent ... The white-haired lady with the red tin can came over to me. "Will you help fight ...? Oh ..." Her mechanical smile vanished and she turned away.

Grabbing her arm, I jerked her to me. "What's the matter? You see something on my face?"

"Why ... mister ... My God, you're hurting my arm!"

"Tell me what you see on my face?"

"See? Nothing. I don't see anything!" she said, hysteria loud in her voice. "I remembered that you contributed before, this morning. That's all."

People were staring at us. I let go of her arm. "Excuse me. I was ... uh ... thinking of something else. Here." I dumped a handful of change in the can.

"Thank you so much." She recovered herself, clumsily tried to pin one of the red buttons on my lapel.

I shoved her hand away. "I already got my badge, the real one."

Walking toward the precinct house I told myself I had to watch it, I damn near hurt the woman. And tomorrow, this smart-aleck specialist would probe and ask a lot of stupid questions. Hell, I never had no confidence in docs, except for Art.

As I walked up the steps of the police station, which looked like all New York City police buildings—older than God—I decided I wasn't going to see the specialist. What could he tell me? What point was there in being sliced open, letting them sample the lousy tumor? It *always* turns out you have it.

The desk man told me Bill was busy but phoned my name in. I stood by the desk and wiped my face, the humidity was as bad as yesterday. I put a couple of mints to work in my mouth and now I could almost *see* the taste, like I was chewing something misty and black.

There was an air of excitement around the precinct. Nothing noticeable, not a lot of activity, but you could sense it. Every time a couple of guys passed the desk they'd be talking with each other in low voices. And there would be a sort of rush in their steps. I waited long enough to finish a mint, blotted the sweat on my face again, asked, "Is Ash alone?"

"I think so, but Lieutenant Ash is very busy and doesn't ..."

I walked back toward the detention cells, past the "Post Condition" board, then up a flight of steps and pushed open Bill's door. He was sitting behind a stack of afternoon papers on his desk, a pair of scissors in his right hand. Although his office only had one small window and Bill was wearing a white-on-white shirt, a brown bow tie, and a double-breasted brown suit, he looked cool. Always a dapper joker, his thin hair was combed back over his almost bald noggin, and he had that youngish look to his puss, like he never had to shave. Except for putting on a little weight and losing a lot of hair, he hadn't changed much in all the years I'd known him.

Looking up from his newspapers, he said, "Hello, Marty. I didn't forget you, I'm busy."

"I see that," I said, sitting down in the other chair in his drab office. "You reduced to cutting out paper dolls?"

"You hear the news?"

"Yeah. I heard about all the news I can take for today." I grinned at him. "So what's new?"

He shook his head slowly. "Marty, I'm in charge of the Detective Squad here. It don't look right for you to be busting in without ..."

"If I hadn't busted into a lot of places when we were partners, you'd still be walking a beat now."

"Maybe," he said softly. And smugly, I thought, as if thinking, But I'm a lieutenant now and you're just a hotel dick in a fourth-rate dive. "But you know how it is, I have to ... well ... keep up a front of authority around here." He waved his hands in the air, as if shoving something aside. "What I mean is, this is a police station, not an old-pals club."

"Looks kind of clubby to me, Bill," I said. "Way all these cops off duty wear sport shirts sticking outside their belts. I remember when you had to dress when going off duty."

"The shirts are cool and they cover a hip holster. That's how the shirt idea started, down in Cuba. Always having revolutions and the lads wore these shirts over their hips to hide the guns they were sporting."

"Sorry I never went to Cuba. They say the fishing is

great down there."

"What the hell we talking about Cuba for?" Bill jabbed a pile of newspapers with his scissors. "It's the damnedest thing, Bochio swore he'd get Cocky, said it a dozen times we know of, yet the sonofabitch has been in Miami for two weeks, locked in a hotel room with his lawyers. Break that alibi!"

"How's Marge and the girls?"

He put the scissors down and stared at me like I was nuts. "They're fine, except Selma has a virus. Look, Marty ..."

"I remember Selma, she's the youngest. Had blond hair, didn't ...?"

"Look, Marty, I'm busy-busy on a murder, so if all you dropped in for was to ask about Marge and the kids, okay, I'll tell them you asked. Now, let me work. Whole damn force is upside down on this one."

"Which one?" I asked, considering making a crack about Bill's pay-off—maybe he thought I came with dough. But he was very touchy about it, blew up if I even talked about it.

Bill sighed. "Wish I was like you, could just ask 'Which one?' Thought you said you heard the news? They found Cocky Anderson's body up in the Bronx this morning, with a .38 slug through his left ear. You know what that means?"

"What?" I asked as if I cared.

"When Bochio first started out as a strong-arm punk, he ran with a gang that used a slug through the left ear as their trademark for people who knew too much. Also, it's an open secret that old Albert swore he'd get Cocky after the jerk made a pass at Bochio's daughter—tried to rape her is the way I heard it. Should be an open-and-shut case, only nothing shuts, nothing even moves. Damn, a tough one has to break in a hot spell like this—I was set to drive the kids up to Orchard Beach this afternoon for a swim."

"If he was killed in the Bronx, where do you come in down here?"

"Your brains die when you buried yourself in that hotel? Marty, you know Cocky Anderson had 'interests' on the docks here. For the love of tears, I have every man I can get my hands on out snooping, canceled all vacations."

"Bochio ain't no hood, and anyway he's been in Miami as you said. Ask me, he's out of the picture. Even that daughter angle is bunk. Cocky was getting too big for the syndicate and they took him out. But the hell with that. I didn't come to talk about rats and punks."

"Just what did you come about, Marty?"

"Oh ... nothing special. Just dropped in to talk."

"About what?"

"What do you mean, about what? Bill, you're the oldest friend I got. Can't a guy drop in to chat with a buddy?"

"Marty, are you sick?"

"Why? Do I look sick?" I asked, and couldn't stop my voice from shaking.

Bill stood up. Except for the little pot belly he was as lean and wiry as ever. "Marty, I don't like to give you a short answer, but I'm up to my eyeballs in work and you breeze in and talk about Cuba, then about the wife and girls, and then you just want to talk. Damnit, Marty, the pressure is on me, real pressure. Some other time we'll talk about old times."

"All right, Bill," I said getting up. "I didn't know you were so busy. Matter of fact I did drop in to talk about Lawrence. He wants to be a cop and I don't want him to have a bad time of it because of me."

Bill sort of groaned and sat down again. "Don't talk

to me about these auxiliary cops. They're driving us nuts."

"Why?"

"Look, if you ask me this is all a lot of crap—if they think New York City might be bombed, then build air-raid shelters, real shelters. In a real bombing what the hell good will a batch of jokers in white helmets do, or all these drills and the rest of it? Ask me, it's just to keep the people on edge. But nobody asks me. The point is some boneheads downtown made a mistake assigning these tin cops here. This is a water-front section. They belong uptown where things are quiet. Don't worry, they won't be here long."

"I thought they had their own setup?"

"They do, up to a point. They got some stuffed do-gooder that's a major or some damn thing in charge of them here, and he's such a strutting jerk, somebody is due to clip him. Most of them are crackpots anyway."

"Lawrence is a bit cop-happy, but otherwise he's a serious kid."

"Marty, I'm not saying they're all jerks, but you know what happens when you get volunteers. Everything is tossed in, including the bottom of the barrel. For every sincere kid like Lawrence, you get a dozen uniform-happy characters who are only looking for a chance to get away from their wives, walk around looking important."

"Me, I don't think there will be a war, but you can never tell. But to get back to Lawrence, watch out for him."

"I will. He's an intelligent kid." Bill looked up at me. "Since when did you get so fatherly over him?"

"Since last night. He wants to be a cop, a real one, and I have a hunch he's eager beaver enough to build himself up, pass the exams. All right, with my name he's starting with two strikes and I don't want him to do anything that will make him look foolish now, when he's on this volunteer-cop kick. Last night he was all excited about some crazy butcher and a phony holdup."

"I know, he came to me with that. He's green and full of too much pep—thinks he has to prove himself, live up to the Bond name, all that. Don't worry—as an auxiliary there isn't much of a jam he can get into."

"He can make a false arrest, like he almost did with that wacky meat chopper. Bill, he's a silly kind of kid and well ... kids today can't take care of themselves the way we did."

"Bull. Marty, the kids today are a lot smarter and tougher than we ever dreamed of being." He stood up again. "Don't worry about him. Couple of weeks and he and the rest of these tin badges will be way uptown, putting in their hours directing traffic, or something. While he's here, I'll keep an eye on him. Marty, when this Anderson mess blows over, I'll have you out for supper some night and we'll talk."

"Marge would sure love that; she could never stand the sight of me. All right, Bill, don't call me, I'll call you," I said, and walked out. I heard him say, "Now, Marty, I told you I'm swamped ..." as I walked down the stairs.

On the way back to the hotel I had a sudden longing for watermelon and stopped in at the corner coffeepot. I told the old-bag waitress to give me a double hunk and she asked, "What you doing, Marty, eating for two?"

"That's it."

She thought it was funny and showed me all her bad teeth in a laugh. "Something as big and ugly as you pregnant!"

"Honey, you don't know how much pregnant," I told

her.

I washed down the bad taste in my mouth with a couple of glasses of iced coffee and I was belching before I reached the hotel lobby. Lawson nodded at the office behind him, said, "Mr. King is quite upset over that rug. He wants you to call him."

"Tell him I couldn't care less," I said, walking past the desk and into the hallway that took me to my room.

There was no sense in stalling. I locked the door and took off my shirt, tie, and shoes—to be comfortable—then I sat down and wrote a short note to Flo telling her about my gut. I didn't know why I wrote her, she wouldn't give a damn. But then I had to leave some sort of note.

I got out my Police Special. A gun can be the most beautiful or the most ugly thing in the world—depending upon which end you're looking at. Right now it looked ugly as hell.

I sat on the bed and put the muzzle in my mouth, tasting the oil. In a few seconds King would have another rug to get himself in an uproar over. For some reason that seemed funny to me.

For the first time in days I smiled—if you can smile with a gun between your teeth—as I pushed the safety off.

Two

At five after ten that night Dewey pounded on my door. I was in a drunken haze—I'd knocked off over a pint in an effort to get up courage and as usual liquor had let me down; all that happened was I went to sleep for a few hours.

I stumbled out of bed and never felt so awful, worse

than when Art told me I had cancer—for the first time in my life I knew I was a phony, a damn coward.

I couldn't understand it; I'd risked my life plenty of times without a thought. I'd even played Russian roulette once when I was young and well crocked. "If you're not afraid to die, then there's nothing to be scared of" was the motto I'd lived by, yet when my own personal chips were down, I didn't have it—I didn't have it at all.

All right, if I didn't have the guts to do it myself, I'd have to figure out some way of getting killed, because I sure wasn't going to take the slow torture of cancer. It wouldn't have been so hard to stop a bullet when I was on the force, but now ... Who the hell bothers shooting a house dick? A lousy ...?

Dewey knocked again, said softly, "Marty, the cop is here, your son."

"All right, all right." I went to the bathroom and washed out the taste in my mouth with tooth powder, ran some water over my face and hands. I slipped on my pants and opened the door. Dewey asked, "What's the matter with you? I been buzzing all night."

"I'm sick." The cold water had done the trick, I was pretty sober.

He looked past me and saw the empty pint beside my bed. "So I see. You're a fine one, not even giving me a taste for my cold. Things went smoothly tonight."

"Yeah?" It was a welcome shock to realize from now on I didn't have to give a damn how anything went— except to figure out a way of dying before the damn cancer got me on a slab.

"Business been pretty fair with the girls. Must be due to it getting a little cooler tonight. What about your son? Don't help things having a cop hanging around the lobby."

"You mean he's in uniform?"

"No, but I know he's a cop. I don't like it."

"Forget him—send him in."

I kicked the fallen soldier under the bed, straightened up the sheets a little, waved a towel around to get the sweaty stink out of the air.

Lawrence came in, said, "The character out at the desk tells me you're sick."

"Heat got me down. Take a chair." The kid had a crew cut like Lawson, was wearing a polo shirt and slacks. He looked better out of uniform. Except for his scrawny neck, he had a neat build for his size.

He slapped my bare stomach. "Still got your rubber tire. Remember how you used to tell about the times you were in the ring and the other guy would waste his punches on your pouch, leave your chin alone, and how you could take it down there all night long?"

I said yeah and looked down at my gut, the fat and the muscles under that, and now under the muscles a lousy tumor waiting like a booby trap. I sat on the bed, changed the subject with, "What's new on Cocky Anderson?" I winked at him. "Speaking of remembering, when you were a young snot you clipped out crime stories like other kids did baseball pictures. What's your dope on this one?"

He winked back. "Okay, keep on riding me, Marty. All I know is what the papers have. Medical examiner claims Anderson had been dead for about twenty-four hours when some youngsters stumbled on his body. The papers say Anderson hadn't been around his usual spots for the last few weeks, but then he'd been a difficult one to keep tabs on. That's about all. Oh yes, they think he was shot someplace else, then dumped in this lot."

"Bochio still shouting off his mouth down in Miami?"

"Sure. The papers have him saying he's sorry somebody beat him to the killing. Bochio's daughter is reported to have collapsed. I suppose you knew Anderson? What is—was—his name, Rocky or Cocky?"

"Both. He came out of the army a pork-and-bean middleweight, but smart enough to give up the ring. Then he became a muscleman, had some luck—sort of a throwback to the old-style trigger-happy hood, except he used his fists. That's when they started calling him Cocky Anderson, way he used to swagger around. For a time he was a syndicate cop, then branched out on his own, bucked them. He was rough—and dumb."

"What's a syndicate cop?" the kid asked—like a kid.

"A punk a little more rugged than the other creeps, keeps them in line. You all out to solve the big murder too, Lawrence, like a movie dick?"

He sat down on the bed beside me. "Gather you don't think much of me as a prospective policeman, do you, Marty?"

"What I think is anybody is a fool to become a cop. Talked to Bill Ash today. He says you volunteer coppers get in his hair, that you're a bunch of screwballs," I said, wondering why I was baiting the kid.

"I wouldn't go that far; we're a fair sampling of any bunch of volunteers. You have the sincere fellows, some jerks, and a few angle lads—wanting to get in on the ground floor, hoping this will be a good thing, money-wise, in time. For the higher-ups, there are some good-paying jobs, the usual political plums."

"Think your night stick will beat an atomic attack?"

He grinned again. "I know what Lieutenant Ash thinks, and in a way he's right—if we really expect a war we should build shelters now. But then, even a little preparedness is better than none at all. Hell, Marty, you know why I'm in it—gives me a taste of being a cop."

"Are you still working on the big liverwurst mystery?"

"Yes. And I'm convinced I've come up with something.

I came to tell you about it. I went up to see where Lande lives. He seems to have come into money recently. The janitor of the building was the talkative type, told me Mrs. Lande has blossomed out with a mink coat and her own Caddy. All within the last month. Before that the janitor claims he had to remind them to come up with the rent."

"You fool, the janitor will tell Lande you were asking about him and he'll complain downtown and they'll take away your tin badge, maybe even arrest you for impersonating a policeman!"

Lawrence gave me a wise smile. "Marty, I'm studying to be a lawyer, I'm aware of the law. I told him I was an insurance investigator making a routine check, and to keep it quiet. The point is, you see what all this proves."

"I don't see nothing."

"It proves he *could* have been robbed of the fifty grand."

"And the two clowns who are supposed to have done it returned it a few hours later with a sorry-opened-by-mistake note!"

Lawrence looked at me like I was backward. "Once we establish that it is possible he had the money, it gives credibility to his original story—that he was robbed. By the way, did you read in the evening papers where two young hoodlums from the West Side were shot to death in a gas-station holdup outside Newark early this morning?"

"I didn't read that, Mr. Holmes. In fact I haven't read the evening papers. But what does it prove?"

"I don't know that it proves anything yet. But struck me it was a coincidence they were both shot through the heart, one bullet each. Fellow has to be quite a marksman to do that in the heat of a stick-up. Another thing, no witnesses."

"There'd hardly be any witnesses early in the morning. When would you expect them to hold up the joint—when it was crawling with customers?"

"Merely a thought," Lawrence said in that precise way he had of talking. "Two young punks rob and return fifty grand, and a dozen hours later two young punks are shot dead. Seems to me the only reason they returned the money would be because they were frightened—frightened of somebody powerful enough to kill them. According to the papers, and I read them all, their description fits the one Lande first gave me of the holdup men. Of course that's a general description. I asked the Newark police to let me see the bodies—they refused. Oh, yes, the gas-station owner has a record, did time for assault many years ago. But he has a permit to carry a gun and he ..."

"You'd better cut this, kid, before you hook up every crime in the country with a robbery that never happened to your batty butcher. I suppose you saw the butcher, asked him to identify the bodies?"

The boy actually blushed. "Why, yes, I did suggest it. I dropped in late in the afternoon, after I read about the killings. You recall I said he was so nervous yesterday? Well, today he was all corny jokes and full of good cheer. Wanted to give me a thick steak. But when I asked him, as a citizen helping the cause of justice, to go over to Newark and look at the bodies, he blew a gasket. Shouted I was trying to make a sick man have another stroke, told me to get out."

"'... *a citizen helping the cause of justice*' ... Goddamn! I— Lawrence, you're one for the books, the joke books!"

"What's the joke? If he was really interested in helping...?"

"Lawrence, first off, nobody likes to look at a couple of stiffs, much less ride all the way over to Newark to do it. Secondly, since the butcher denied there ever was a holdup, why should he agree to look at a couple of dead punks?"

"There're two sides to every coin and the reverse side of this one is that Lande is scared, that he knows the two dead men are the same ones who robbed him. Okay, laugh if you wish, but that's my opinion of the case. I think there's something in all this. Tomorrow I'm going to have a talk with Lande's driver."

"I hope you're not giving this cock-and-bull story to Bill Ash."

"He's too busy on the Anderson killing to see me." He stood up. "Dot was glad I talked to you yesterday."

"Was she? Has she changed much?"

"No. At least not that I've noticed or ..." He saw my gun on the dresser. I'd forgotten all about the lousy thing. "What are you doing with this—planning to kill somebody?"

"If I say yes, will you tie me up with your liverwurst tycoon? That's what guns are for, mostly to bluff and sometimes to kill—if you can."

He went over and hefted the gun, balanced it with one finger under the trigger guard. I said, "Forget that and tell me more about Dot."

"She's the same. We don't have guns. Marty, is this your old gun?"

"Aha."

"Sure seen plenty of action. Where are your citations, Marty?"

"I don't know, probably around someplace. You medal-happy?"

He opened the top drawer, put the gun in. "Marty, please stop treating me like the village idiot. I want to be a good cop—if I can—and a live one. If I find anything new from Lande's driver, I'll drop in tomorrow night, if you don't mind."

"Lawrence, I told you I don't mind. And keep away from your butcher—mind your own business."

"We differ on what is my business. But I'll be careful."

I shrugged. "All right, and if the joker offers you a steak again, bring it here if you don't want it."

"Petty bribes, the curse of law enforcement," he said, mocking me.

"You ain't kidding—hold out for the big ones," I told him, going over to my desk to make sure the note I'd written Flo wasn't in sight. "Like a drink?"

"No thanks. I have to get home, early class tomorrow."

I walked him to the door and as we shook hands he said, "Leave the bottle alone, Marty. Get some sleep."

"Think you're big enough to be giving me advice, kid?"

"I don't have to be big to see you look tired. So long, Marty."

When he left I felt lousy. Lawrence was a jerk, but a nice jerk, one of these serious kids, and not as silly as he sounded. Only that kind gets hurt as bad as the wild ones. Damn, my own son comes in and all we can talk about is killings and stick-ups. I should have talked to him more—but about what? He was a stranger to me. That was the damn trouble —I'd lived all my life among strangers.

I was hungry and my gut hurt. The quiet of the room gave me the spooks. I was lonely. I turned on my table radio and listened to some jazz, but that didn't help. I phoned Dewey, told him to send Barbara in.

"Now? It's early—can't you wait?"

"Send her in and shut up!" I unlocked my closet and took out another pint. I had four cases stacked there—

late at night when a guy wanted a bottle real bad, a pint brought five to ten bucks. I never made much on liquor though, because I was always my own best customer.

I opened the bottle, washed out two glasses, lit a cigarette. After a few puffs the smoke tasted sour and I threw the cigarette away, chewed some mints.

When Barbara knocked on the door I told her to come in, and she asked, "What's up?"

"Nothing."

"Is that so?" she said, giving me a wise look.

"It's so. Want a shot?"

"Small one. Hear you ain't feeling so chipper."

"I can't sleep," I said, pouring her a shot.

"It's the lousy heat." She put the drink down with one fast gulp, sat on the bed. "Come on, schoolboy, I'll relax you."

"Cut it. Let's talk. What do you plan to do? I mean, hell you know you only have another few years left in this racket, then what?"

She jumped to her feet. "What kind of talk is that?"

"Friendly talk. You and me, we don't have to kid each other. Let's talk about something else. Where do you come from—a farm?"

"Are you nuts? This is the best time of the night. I can't sit here and bull with you while the other girls are turning all the tricks. I have to make ..."

"Let your pimp buy his new Caddy a day later!" I said, reaching over and slapping her. I didn't hit Barbara hard, but her left cheek went dead white, then a flaming red as she fell on the bed and began to sob.

I sat beside her, held her in my arms. "I'm sorry, honey. Sorry as hell."

"What's got into you, Marty?" she asked, crying into the gray hairs on my chest. "What the hell's the matter with you?"

"I'm on edge, can't sleep. I ... Look, I'm real sorry. You know how things is with you and me. I got no use for those other whores, but you ..."

"Don't call me that!"

"Why not? You are a whore and I'm an ex-cop turned pimp and ... Stop bawling. Told you I'm sorry. I lost my head." It felt pretty swell holding her, feeling her crying. Somehow it made me feel alive.

She pushed out of my arms, dried her face with a sheet. "I can't stand a guy hitting me. And you ..."

I put my hand over her mouth. Her face looked tired and drawn, played out. "Barbara, how many times must I tell you I didn't mean to hit you?" I put my hand in my pants pocket, took out a bill. Happily it was only a five spot. "If I give you this will you buy yourself some perfume, stockings, or something—keep it out of Harold's mitts?"

"I can't hold out any dough on him. You know how funny he is about that. And you don't have to pay me ..."

"I'm not paying you. This is a present."

"Then buy me some perfume—give me the bottle not the dough."

"All right."

She got off the bed, looked at herself in the mirror. "I got to go now, fix my face up."

I walked her to the door and then took a stiff drink—had a hard time keeping it down. The news came on the radio, all about the Anderson killing. I shut it off and walked around the room for a while, trying to think. I opened the drawer and stared at my gun—knew I couldn't do it. It was crazy—there were plenty of mugs around who would be hysterical to plug me if I told them to, only how do you tell a slob you want him to kill you? How do you look? What do you say? What ...?

The door opened and I slammed the drawer shut. Barbara came in. "I got some sleeping pills here. Two—enough to knock you out."

"I never fooled with goof balls."

"Won't do you no harm and will make you sleep like a baby," she said, filling a glass with water.

I washed the pills down. "How long before they work?"

"Few minutes, if you don't fight them. Lie down and relax."

I sat on the bed and wondered if this might be it. Take a box of the junk and slip out of this world. Only somebody would be sure to wake me, or find me, in the Grover. I could get a box and go to another hotel where ...

"Feel sleepy?"

"Not yet. And stop watching me like you thought I was getting ready to explode or disappear."

"You got to stretch out, meet the pills halfway." She gave me an odd little smile. "You're a crazy guy, Marty. Are you afraid to kiss me?"

"Hell, no," I said.

I gave her a big hug and kiss, glad I had the mint taste in my mouth. She flicked her tongue at the tip of my nose, said coyly, "That was sweet, Marty," then she kissed me hard, threw her tongue halfway down my throat. When she pulled away she gave me a smart grin, said, "We're alike. I'm in a lonely business, dealing with lonely people who want to get rid of me fast as they can. A cop's the same way—nobody wants him except when they need him. For a time your being even an ex-cop made me uneasy."

"What are you, the wise old bird tonight?"

"Sometimes I like you, like you a lot. Now hit the sack."

I stretched out on the bed and Barbara waved from

the door. I told her, "Fix the door so it will lock."

She did that, waved again, closed the door. I loosened my belt, reached over and turned off the light. And waited, wondering if I was going to dream of Mrs. De-Costa again. I started thinking about Lawrence.

I could have talked to the boy about fishing. Once I took him surf casting with me, and he loved it but he caught a bad cold being up all night on the beach. I even let him take a slug of whiskey. What I remember most is the big bass I got, about sixteen pounds. Had a fight pulling him in and Lawrence was excited too. In the morning when we were getting ready to go, I took a fillet out of the fish, left the rest, and the kid said, "You shouldn't do that, he was such a beautiful fish."

"I'm not going to lug any stinking sixteen-pound fish on a train."

Lawrence was thin and sort of sissy looking and he wailed, "But to leave him on the beach like this, all open, it isn't fair to the fish!"

"Fair? The bass is dead. And what the hell does a fish know about fair or unfair?"

The little drip started crying and then sneezing, and when I got him home Dot bawled the devil out of me. Worrying over a fish, now over a nutty butcher who ...

The next thing I knew I was jerking myself erect and there was sunlight in the room. The damn radio was still on and the three o'clock news was starting. It reminded me of the old days when I'd pound my ear for a dozen or more hours, sleeping off a drunk.

My mouth was cracking dry and there was a dull, uneasy feeling in my gut. I felt dopey instead of rested. And it was another hot day. A cold shower snapped me out of it a bit. Then I shaved, washed my teeth a couple of times—they seemed to be coated—found a clean shirt and dressed. I chewed a pack of gum for my breath.

Dewey was behind the desk already, looking red-eyed, the veins in his nose large. He asked, "Howya feeling, Marty?"

"Hungry as a church rat. What are you doing in so early?"

"Lawson wanted a couple hours off—going to some art exhibit. As if the heat isn't bad enough, one of the maids didn't show, called in sick."

"Which one—Lilly?"

He nodded.

"Dewey, what was the number yesterday?"

"Let's see ... I think a six was leading ... I only play the single action ... and ... yes, I recall now, it was 605. You have anything down?"

"Think I did." I went into the office and found Lilly's home address.

As I came out, Dewey said, "Marty, you and I get along because we both mind our own business, so if what I'm going to say is out of line, say so. The thing is, you're acting kind of funny."

"You mean I'm for laughs?"

"Don't kid me, Marty. Mr. King is up in the air, wanted to talk to you and wore out his hand knocking on your door."

"Tell Mr. King I may achieve a sudden ambition in life—busting his weasel face."

Dewey blinked his watery eyes. "Got another job?"

"Nope."

"Tell you, Marty, we run the hotel so smoothly I wouldn't like to see you lose this one—have to break in a new man. Lucky for you there wasn't any trouble last night. Another thing, a Dr. Dupre has been calling you, three times in the last hour. I would say he was kind of angry at you, too."

"Long as I have a buddy-buddy like you, Dewey pal,

what have I to worry about?" I said, walking out.

At the coffeepot I had a couple of pastrami sandwiches and some orange juice. My stomach was solid and I felt good. I was a dummy not to have thought of sleeping pills. Merely rent a room in one of the uptown hotels where I wasn't known, tell them not to disturb me. About fifteen straight hours would do the trick.

I felt so good I listened to the old waitress's dirty jokes—which she told me over and over again every week—and nearly gave her heart condition by leaving a half-a-buck tip.

I had close to three grand in a safe-deposit box and another grand in a savings account. I had to leave it to somebody. Leaving it to Lawrence would be a waste; he'd never learn how to enjoy a buck. Flo would get hysterical if I left her anything. Barbara really needed the dough, but it would only end up as a new car for pimp Harold. Still, best I draw up a will or some snotty cousins in Atlantic City would come into it—if they were still alive. The last time I saw them I was twenty-one and they gave me a crummy stickpin.

I walked around till I found a public typist—a pimply girl in a plumbing store. I dictated a short will giving Lawrence all my dough on the condition he buy Dewey a barrel of cheap wine. I asked the girl if she was a notary and she told me, "Wills do not need to be notarized, just two witnesses."

"Okay, you want to be a witness?"

"I don't mind," she said and called some guy out of the shop in the back of the store. He signed as a witness too, getting the paper all dirty with his greasy hands. The girl even made him put his address down. All this cost me only a buck and I took the will back to the Grover and left it in a sealed envelope in my desk.

Across from the Grover there's an old drugstore which

I give all the hotel business. I dropped in there and Sam said, "Marty, don't tell me you need a new supply so soon."

"I want to buy a small bottle of perfume. Something going for about three bucks. Wrap it up nice."

"What kind?"

"How would I know? Anything that smells strong."

Sam showed me a bottle that was all glass with about four drops of yellow liquid that looked like a doctor's sample. "This is the real stuff, from Paris and no lie."

"All right. By the way, Sam, I get calls for sleeping pills now and then. Let me have a box of goof balls."

Sam reached under the counter, then showed me a tiny box. "These are the newest thing on the market. Put you to sleep but no drugs, no chance of anything going wrong."

"I want the old kind, the strong ones."

"Marty, you don't understand, these are safe. You can take the whole box and your heart won't burst, or your lungs get paralyzed."

"Sam, I want goof balls."

He had heavy lids and when he got excited the lids seemed to droop, giving him an evil expression. "Marty, you need a doctor's prescription for those."

"Stop horsing around. Sam, you know me. When a guy asks for a pill, pays for it, I have to give him what he wants. Don't worry, I won't give him more than two. Think I want to get into trouble?"

"But they're damn strict these days. I can lose my license, my store, maybe worse."

"You put them in a plain box—I found them in one of the rooms when a guest checked out."

"Marty, you have no idea how tight they are on sleeping pills and sedatives. I can't take the chance." His fat face was troubled, his eyes nearly shut.

"All right, if you want me to start dealing with another
…"

"Marty, be reasonable!"

"I'm asking you for a simple favor and you're making
a production out of it. What's wrong with you, Sam?
You think I'd be nuts, giving some clown too many?"

The lids opened a little and after a moment he whispered, "Okay, but remember, if anything happens, I'll
swear you never got them here."

Sam went behind the clouded glass partition in the
rear of his store, returned in a few minutes with a plain
pillbox which he crudely palmed in my hand as we
shook hands—although we were alone in the store. He
said, "No charge. Just pay for the perfume. You can
have that wholesale—a dollar seventy-three."

"How many pills are in here?"

"A dozen. I'll cover it in my inventory—somehow."

"To be on the safe side, what's a fatal dose?"

"Marty, don't talk like that!"

"Hell, Sam, I got to know."

"Well, never give more than two during a twelve-hour
period. Maybe three if the party looks young, but not
even one if the party is old and looks like his ticker is
shot."

"Would five or six taken at one time kill?"

"Marty, what are you saying? Suppose somebody over-
heard us! Any time you give a party five or six at one
time, leave town fast."

"All right, and thanks. Don't worry, Sam."

I took the subway uptown and got myself in the rush
hour, so I was all sweaty when I shoved my way out at
Ninety-sixth Street. I took a three-buck room in a large
hotel on One Hundredth Street, but not big enough to
sport a house dick. I registered under my own name,
said I came from Jersey City, paid in advance for two

days.

It was a better room than any we had at the Grover. My stomach started rumbling and when that was over I sat on the bed and stared at the light brown walls—there's nothing as lonely as a hotel room. I wanted to see Flo. I went down to the lobby and tried looking her up in the phone book, but she might have married half a dozen times since I last saw her.

I walked along Broadway, considered going up to see Lilly and getting my dough, only what did I need dough for now? Still, I didn't like for people to put something over on me. The neighborhood had changed. When I worked out of the precinct on One Hundredth Street, it used to be all micks with a lot of Jews. Now it was full of spicks.

I was walking around like a damn tourist, so I took a cab down to the Fifty-second Street night club. It was near seven and a porter was sweeping up, taking the chairs off the tables. A roly-poly bartender was washing glasses, getting ready for the night. He looked at me nervously, asked, "What can I do for you?" He had a fat face and an even fatter mouth. When he talked, it looked like his head was coming off.

"I want the home address of Flo Harris," I said, the proper growl in my voice.

"Flo? Flo who?"

"Come on, fatso, the 'Divine Flame,' one of your strippers."

"She'll be here about ten and you can ..."

"I want to see her now."

"You a cop?" His voice was a bull whisper.

"What do I look like?"

"A cop." He sighed. "If she's in a jam we'll cancel her act right ..."

"She ain't in trouble. But I need to see her—now."

"I'll see if I can locate her."

He waddled from behind the bar over to a door and a second later some drip who looked like a younger Mr. King stuck his sharp puss out of the office and gave me the eye. When the barkeep returned a moment later he told me she was living in a Forty-sixth Street hotel and her name was Mrs. Flo York.

I told him, "All right. Don't phone her I'm coming, or I'll close you up."

"You got us wrong—we always co-operate with the police. We have to. Care for a shot?"

"No. But I'll take a mint leaf."

"A mint *leaf?*"

"Sure, my mother was frightened by a cow."

He put a few leaves on a plate and I walked out chewing them.

The hotel was one of these ratty dumps you find in the Times Square area, worse than the Grover because it suffered more daily wear and tear. Flo was in 417. As I knocked on the door I wondered if I'd have to throw "Mr. York" out.

Flo looked great when she opened the door. She was wearing a light print dress that sort of showed off the curves without bragging about them. Her face was minus make-up and except for a few lines around her eyes, she hadn't aged. She said, "Marty!" Said it big and her teeth showed her real age.

"Hello, Flo. Can I come in?"

She stepped aside and it was a seedy room, the walls with old dirty rose wallpaper—bedbug traps—and space enough for a crummy metal bed, a small dresser covered with bottles and jars of cosmetics, one skinny chair, a metal bed table, and clothing piled atop her two suitcases in the corner.

Flo had on low-heeled shoes, the way I always liked

her best, and her long black hair hung off the back of her head in a horse's tail. She waved a hand at the room. "Not much, hey, Marty?"

I smiled, took some underthings off the chair and sat down. I tossed the things on the bed. Flo always was sloppy. I had a feeling I was home.

She stared at me with hard, suspicious eyes, said sarcastically, "Make yourself comfortable!"

"I did. You haven't changed a bit, not even the acid in your voice."

"What's on your mind, Marty?" She looked around for a cigarette. I dug in my pockets, didn't have a pack. She finally found some on the dresser, lit one as she held out the pack to me.

I shook my head.

Flo blew a cloud of smoke in my face. "Used to be a chain smoker, Marty. What's the matter, believe this lung-cancer stuff?"

"Lost my taste. Who's afraid of lung cancer?" I said, laughing—my own little joke I was stuck with.

She puffed a few more times, waiting, then asked, "What do you want?"

"Not a thing. Merely dropped in to see you. Saw your picture in front of the club and got your address. Where did you get the York handle?"

"Left that louse couple of years ago. Didn't I read about you being bounced from the force?"

"Aha. But they fixed it so I retired on physical disability, said I was 'nervous.' I saw you in the movies a couple of times."

She sat on the bed. Aside from a few tiny veins starting to show, her legs were as perfect as ever.

"Come up to see my legs, Marty?" she asked, raising her skirt.

"Don't think so. I could drop into the club if I wanted

to see them."

She ran her eyes over my clothes, my shoes. "If you came for a handout, you're wasting time."

"I never held my hand out to you. Told you I'm on a pension. And I have a two-bit job. You need a couple of bills?"

"You giving me something? That's a twist. Come on, Marty, I have a show to make. What's this all about?"

"Nothing. Wanted to see you, talk to you. Lately I got to thinking about us, the way it was real fine—at the start."

She puffed on her butt like an engine. "Selling something, Marty?"

"What's wrong with a joker getting a yen to see his ex-wife? Here." I took out Barbara's perfume. "I brought you a little gift."

Flo stared at the tiny package as if she expected it to snap at her, then slowly opened the gift wrapping, said, "Oh, it's some Clichy! This is real sweet of you."

"Nothing much—ten bucks."

"Ten bucks your ass but it's the nicest gift I ever got," Flo said quickly, and for a moment I thought she was either going to cry or put on an act. Her hand hugged the bottle. "Marty, you really do want to see me."

"Sure. What's the matter—don't guys chase you any more?"

"I don't mean that. Would you believe it, Marty, I was thinking about you recently, too."

"No, I wouldn't believe it."

She suddenly laughed and crushed the cigarette, came over and sat on my lap. "You're still the same mean son-of a-bitch, the only stud I ever knew who didn't bull me, took me as I was."

"Sometimes you were quite a lot, Flo," I said, opening the back of her dress, then giving up the idea. It felt swell having Flo on my lap, smelling her, talking to her.

"I know, sometimes we were real good, and then other times ..." She nibbled at the lobe of my ear, the right one that used to be cauliflowered. "Marty, I'm sick of a lot of things. Lousy hotel rooms, stale night-club dressing rooms. I'm sick of climbing. I was foolish, never even knew exactly what I was aiming for."

"You mean you're getting on. You were all right, Flo, except you never stopped bouncing."

"And you, you never bounced at all, a big solid lump, proud of your fists, like a kid."

"Guess so, ambition never bothered me."

She took my hands and pressed them over her breasts. I remembered now how we used to joke in bed—I'd press her nipples and say, "Special delivery." Flo put her head back on my shoulder, said, "I've had it, Marty, had it over my head." She paused. "I have time, want to go to bed?"

"Maybe later. Let's talk."

"Since when did you get to be a talker?"

"Since a few days ago."

"Your hands are still so rough and strong, so good. Isn't it nutty, an ugly buzzard like you still sending me? Oh, Marty, I'm not bulling you, I have been thinking of you."

"What were you thinking?" I asked as a belch tore at my guts. I turned my head and let the gas out slowly.

"I'm done in show biz, I'm going no place but down now. Another year and I won't even be able to get these stinking dates. I got me a big house out on Long Island, way out, near Montauk. It can be fixed up so we have about thirty rooms. I have a couple living there now, keeping it up—and keeping me broke. That's why I'm living in this dumpy hotel."

"How did you get the place?" I asked, stroking her

long hair. It was very soft and her neck and shoulders were as firm as an athlete's.

"A fan of mine got pie-eyed one week end, gave it to me. Don't worry, it's all mine, I have the deed. I've been holding it over a year, waiting for somebody like you. Marty, the two of us could move out there, make it into a first-class hotel."

"I've got a head start along those lines—I'm a hotel dick."

She clapped her hands. "An omen! A sign we should be back together!"

"You still go in for star reading, palms, and all that other junk?"

"Seriously, Marty, we can make a go of it, live well. That's all I want out of life from now on, to live graciously. I've seen how some of these rich cats do it, and this hotel will be our meal ticket. We hire a man and wife to cook and clean the rooms. I have it all planned— it will be a kind of joint where people come to rest, take it easy. No kids, no drunks. Expensive but not ritzy. Get what I mean—fine food, quiet, lounging around the beach, fishing. And we'll live just like the guests. We won't get rich but nobody breaks their back either. Buy it?"

"Sounds great. I wouldn't mind a lot of sun and sleeping late."

Flo squirmed on my lap. "Marty, all we need is a couple of grand worth of good furniture. I'll do the decorating and you be a handy-Andy. I'll make you a one-third partner."

"Nope, not for me."

Her voice rose. "You said it sounded great. What the hell you want—half? Okay, make it fifty-fifty. I know enough rich johns and toney theatrical people we can get as a starter. Then in time, we build up the ..."

"Honey, I can't do it."

"Damn you, Marty, I'm not asking you for any dough. The joint is free and clear. I can raise a few grand on it from any bank. Hell, I can sell it any time I want for nearly forty thousand!"

"Flo, you don't understand. I'd go for the deal without any partnership, even put up the dough. The trouble is, it's too late for me."

"What makes it ...? Hey! Marty, you married, got kids?"

"Nope, you were the last Mrs. Bond. It's something else."

"What else can it be?" Flo asked, making a bra out of my hands.

I didn't answer and she gave me a know-it-all smile, then reached over and picked up the perfume from the bed. She opened the bottle and put a few drops behind each ear, then pulled her dress off her shoulders. "I go with the house, too, Marty. You know that. This time it will be for keeps. I still have time to try for a kid, if you want."

The damn perfume smelled like lilies of the valley, the flowers they have at funerals. I lifted Flo off my lap, sat her on the bed—the sure smile was still on her face.

The perfume stink gave me the creeps, like death was following me around. I felt the box of goof balls in my pocket, headed for the door. "So long, Flo, it was nice seeing you."

"Marty!" She came running across the room, grabbed my coat. "Marty, what's the matter, what did I say wrong?"

"You said everything right. It's a good offer, so is your bed. And we'd make a go of the hotel, probably be very happy leading a nice slow life, grow old gracefully, and all that slop."

"Why is that slop?"

"It isn't, it's great, only I can't make it." Taking her hands off my sleeve, I opened the door. "I'll be dead by Saturday. 'Bye, Flo."

Walking down the hall to the elevator I wondered why I had to be such a dramatic ham. I felt lousy. And it would be good out there with Flo, away from crummy hotels, the smell of insecticide, watching people. We'd have a station wagon and I'd meet the trains, maybe tend the desk, and knock off for a few hours of surf fishing anytime I wanted. It was a great buy—for a healthy joker.

I stood outside the hotel for a while. It was a bit cooler. I walked over to Broadway, stared at all the cheap gaudy lights, the hicks—from out of town and in town—walking up and down the Stem, enjoying all this phony sparkle, the tough kids in jeans and black leather windbreakers who needed a belt in the slats—or something to do. At one time Broadway used to give me a bang, now it looked like a freak show.

I stopped and had a couple of hot dogs, a coconut drink, then walked uptown. I kept looking around like a stranger, feeling terribly dramatic and sorry for myself—and knowing I was enjoying every second of it. It was like there were two of me—one guy saying, "Look around, get a full whiff of this." And the other saying, "Cut it, there's nothing left but to go to the hotel room, take the sleeping pills and you've had it."

I stared into each passing face, hoping I'd see somebody I knew. Maybe a jerk from the army, a ... I suddenly remembered Art. At least I ought to call him. I reached him at his home and he started bawling me out, adding, "He'll soak you double now for missing your appointment. What happened to you?"

"Nothing."

"I've been calling you at your hotel but ..."

"Thanks for being interested, Art, but I'm not going to that specialist."

"You're not? What do you mean by that?"

"I've become a Christian Scientist—I'm not going to let any doc monkey with my belly."

"You must be crocked. Listen to me, Marty, this isn't anything to clown about. I advise you to ..."

I tried to laugh. "Why not clown about it, Art? Told me yourself it was nothing to worry about. Tumor-shumor. Look, kid, don't worry about me. I'm taking care of it another way."

"Have you been to another doctor?"

"No, you're my doctor. I'm trying an old-fashioned remedy. Thanks for everything, Art. And don't worry about me."

"Marty, stop acting like a thick-headed ..."

I hung up, bought a paper and took a cab uptown. It gave me a queer feeling to realize I wouldn't need the sixty-odd bucks I had in my wallet, could throw them out the window if I wanted.

There wasn't much in the paper. They had already started the life story of Cocky Anderson, and some broad had come forward and said she was his wife and they had a baby boy. There was a picture of a plain-faced woman named Pollard who had backed her husband against a wall—with a Chevvy. Somehow her face looked familiar and I read the whole piece. They'd had a spat and he'd run to her mother's—he was one guy who was on the best of terms with his mother-in-law. Mrs. Pollard was driving by when she saw him leaving and he tried to duck into the driveway, so she wouldn't see him. She swung the Chevvy into the driveway and chased him down to the dead-end wall of the garage door. She said she didn't know "why I did it. But I feel relieved now."

Her face still looked like somebody I knew, but I couldn't place it. I looked through the paper to see if they'd caught Mr. Mudd, the amateur stick-up artist, but he'd faded from the news.

There was a column about past baseball greats who hadn't made the Hall of Fame and an editorial about crime followed by another hash about New York City gangsters lolling around Miami. Bochio's alibi was perfect. Not only did he claim he'd been in his hotel room for two weeks, but the Miami police had a two-man guard on his room twenty-four hours a day during those weeks.

Several minor hoods had been picked up and questioned. There was the usual statement from Homicide about "waiting for a break in the case ... any hour now ..."

I turned back and looked at the snap of Mrs. Pollard. She had nice eyes. Had they looked so nice when she was bearing down on hubby with the Chevvy?

We reached the hotel and I gave the cabbie a dime tip, wondered why I didn't hand him all my dough, or at least a buck.

Up in my room I undressed to my shorts, lit a cigarette, and decided there wasn't any point in horsing around. I dropped all the pills but two into a glass of water, hoped they wouldn't have a bad taste.

I never found out.

For an hour I sweated as I tried to lift that little glass to my mouth, but it was like a great weight—I couldn't get it off the table. It was exactly like with the gun, when I didn't have the strength to squeeze the trigger. I moved my arms, my hands, but not when they were holding the glass. I strained and I sweated and cried with shame, yet nothing helped—I didn't have the guts to take my life.

I couldn't understand it; I'd never lacked the old moxie before. Even in the ring, when I started going against some of the real pros, the dancing masters, who cut and hacked at me for ten rounds while I kept moving in, waiting for one shot—even then when I knew I was outclassed and being stupid-brave, still I had the guts to keep going.

I tried and tried lifting the glass, then I finally knocked it over trying to lift it with my teeth, and my muscles loosened up. I sat down, staring at the wet spot on the rug for a long time, thinking of nothing, of everything. I could practically see my arms bone thin as a doc hunted for a spot to stick the intravenous-feeding needle.

I stared at the rug so long I got a bit slappy; I suddenly saw Mrs. DeCosta screaming at me, heard the shrill "*You thug with a badge!*" I saw the blood streaming from her nose, a tiny pink trickle.

Closing my eyes made her go away, and then I had the runs and forgot about everything. I was sweating pretty badly and was very weak as I sat on the side of the bed and smoked a butt—for three puffs. As a kind of experiment I took a single pill and was able to swallow that. However when I started reaching for the second one, the last one, my arm wouldn't move. It was so damn uncanny I nearly started praying.

The one pill didn't do a thing but put me in a sort of haze—and I had a head start on that. I stretched out on the bed and wasn't asleep, at least I don't think I was. I stared up at the darkness and for no reason lazily ran through my life.

Right from Mom's funeral, and her looking so cold and different in the cheap casket, so different from the way she was gay and full of jokes in our room. Then moving in with Aunt May, and all the times I ran away from that silly old bitch with her big house and a million rules about "Don't do that!" She meant well, I guess, but an old-maid bitch is the worst kind. And the three years in the "home." Some home! I was more muscular than the average ten-year-old and I learned two things in the home. Many times a day I found out I was a bastard—till I teed off on a big kid—and also learned I could punch.

On the TV screen that was my mind I saw the semi-pro sand-lot football games, how I lived all week on the ten or fifteen bucks I made as a tackle—if we won. The bootleg boxing bouts when a carload of us "amateurs" would tour in a battered heap from New York to Albany, Utica, Buffalo, Toronto, Montreal, Binghamton—fighting each night under a phony name, returning to New York with a hundred bucks or more in our pockets, sure we owned the world.

Suddenly the girls passed on the screen of my brain— the first one I went with, up in Syracuse, and I was older than I should have been. Then all the other babes— blurred faces and figures. If I had left the gals alone I might have got someplace in the ring. I was a lot like Tony Galento in build and style. But that's slop, I was always an alley fighter—ring rules bothered my style, slowed me to a walk.

The crazy thing was, the next thing I knew I was sitting up in bed, as if an alarm clock had gone off. I felt rested and full of pep. The room gave me the spooks. I showered and cleaned out my mouth. It was only 4:30 A.M. when I tossed my key at the sleepy desk clerk. He asked, "Leaving so early?" as he dived for the registration card.

"Don't worry, I'm paid—for two days. I'm done with the room. Use it for a crap game if you like."

I walked down to Ninety-sixth Street and took the subway. The hot, stale air of the train took away my good mood. There was a creepy-looking case sitting opposite me—looked like a junkie. I sat down and pretended I was sleeping. I'd read where these punks often knifed a drunk as they rolled him.

I sat there waiting, watching, wondering if I'd try to stop the knife, like I did the pills and the gun. Then I was full of this cold fear that I wouldn't be able to die soon enough, would end up a lingering corpse in a hospital.

We were alone most of the time, but my creep didn't move. At my station I got off, feeling kind of childish, and walked over to the Grover. It was a little after five.

When Dewey saw me he asked in a whisper, "Where the hell you been?" He didn't sound like he'd been sleeping much, looked more red-eyed than usual.

"On the town, having a gay old time."

"Jeez, whole damn town's been looking for you. That Doc Dupre has been calling all night. Then the cops been calling you, a Lieutenant Ash. And she's been waiting for you most of the evening."

I followed his skinny, shaking finger, saw Dot curled up in one of the leather chairs. She wasn't asleep; her eyes were big and tired. She looked about the same, small and plump. And her clothes were still the kind of rags she had to wear because it was against the law to go nude. Style and sharp dressing were things Dot never bothered with.

As I walked toward her I saw the eyes were puffed from crying. Curled up, she looked smaller than ever. I pulled a chair over, sat down. "What's wrong, Dot?"

"Lawrence was beaten up, badly. He may die."

"What? the kid ...? When?"

"Late this—yesterday afternoon." Her voice was almost lifeless, and she seemed in a state of shock. "He'd volunteered for duty and he was beaten up on his way to the station house."

"Where is he now?"

"Emergency ward, St. Vincent's. Marty, you must help us."

"All right. What does the kid need, blood?" Would they take mine when I told them about the cancer?

"They're taking care of him. That isn't it. Marty, they killed Mac. I couldn't stand it if I lost my Lawrence!" Her voice quickened and she took my hand, clung to it so hard her nails cut me.

"I know how you feel. I'm sure the cops will ..."

"No, Marty! I want you to do it."

I stroked her hand. "Do what?"

"Marty, I don't know if I'm crazy or what. I know revenge is stupid and wrong, but all I've been able to think about since this happened is—I want you to get whoever did this. Marty, at times you're good and kind, and at other times you're mean and cruel, vicious—I'm appealing to the mean streak in you, your nasty side—get whoever did this so he'll never be able to hurt another Lawrence again!"

"All right. How bad is the kid?"

"Still on the critical list, but they say he has a chance. He's calling for you." She dug her nails into my palm again. "Marty, you'll do this for me, for Lawrence?"

"Yes. I told you I would."

She dropped my hand, stood up, said simply, "Thank you, Marty," and headed toward the door.

I ran after her. "Where are you going?"

"Home. I'm very tired." Her voice was dead, listless.

"I'll get you a cab."

"Don't bother. Marty, turn your strength, your cruelty, your toughness to some good—find out who did this."

"All right, all right, but let me get you a cab."

We stopped a cruising taxi over on Winter Street and

she gave him an address way uptown and I slipped him five bucks, told him to take her directly there.

As the taxi drove off, I had a mouthful of bile, or something that tasted bitter as hell. I had my own troubles, and now this.

I spat the bitter stuff out and walked toward St. Vincent's Hospital.

Three

At the hospital a doctor told me, "It's good you've come, Mr. Bond, he keeps asking for you. Perhaps if you spoke to him for a few seconds, he'll relax and go to sleep. Sleep is so important for him."

"How bad is he?"

"Off the critical list, temporarily. He's been beaten up by a professional, if you know what I mean. In the space of seconds he received a concussion and a nasty scalp cut—from a gun butt no doubt—a broken nose, broken eardrum, and internal injuries. I imagine after he was knocked down he was stomped upon—he has what appears to be a small rupture of the left kidney plus several broken ribs. That's all we've been able to find, so far. He's passing blood in his urine which could mean other injuries beside the kidney."

"Can he talk?"

"Oh, yes. He's under a sedative, but continues to fight sleep, has been asking for you all night. Let him talk himself out and say nothing that will excite him."

"All right."

He took me into the kid's room, and Lawrence was just another body in a white bed, his head and face wrapped in bandages like a mummy. The doc left and when I said, "Hello, Lawrence," the bandages moved and a small voice asked, "Marty? Marty?"

"Yes, kid."

"Dad! I've been waiting for you such a long long time." The voice sounded terribly tired.

"I just heard. Now take it ..."

"Marty, it doesn't matter. But this has to be tied up with the butcher. You see that?" There was more strength in his voice now.

"Looks like it, Lawrence."

"See, we auxiliary cops ... there're fewer of us.... The fellows think the police department isn't ... They think we're a joke. Point is, I happened to call in. There was a cop without a partner scheduled to do patrol duty, so I volunteered to come in. I was walking through a side street; I'd come down by the Fifth Avenue bus. I passed a hallway and a voice called out, 'Officer! Officer!' When I stepped inside I was hit over the head."

"See anything of who did it?"

"No. I caught just a glimpse of a man who looked—don't laugh—he looked like Dick Tracy. When he was kicking me I must have come to for a moment. I remember him saying *'Bastid! Bastid!'* with a sort of growl ... a hiss."

"How about the voice that called you, man or woman?"

"A ... a false voice." The words dragged out.

"Lawrence, you're sure he said *bastid*, not *bastard?*"

"Bas ... tid."

He was either sleeping or had passed out. I pressed the buzzer on the bed table and the doc came in. After looking over the kid, the doc tugged at my arm. I nodded but didn't move. I had a feeling, a hunch, about who'd worked the kid over—although it was a crazy hunch. As I stood there a sense of relief came over me. If I was right—about the hunch—he was the roughest monkey in the business. And he'd be my boy too, for if I went after him I wouldn't have to worry much about living—especially if I was a little careless.

The doc said, "Might as well go now, Mr. Bond. He'll sleep for ten hours or more, I hope."

I nodded and when we stepped outside his room there was a cop—a real cop—on a chair tilted against the wall, smoking a cigarette. He was a tall, lean cop, a youngster. I asked, "You guarding this room?"

He nodded.

"Where the hell were you when I went in?"

"Stretching my legs, but I had my eye on the room."

"Your eye isn't what's wanted—we want you and your gun on the door!"

"I saw you come in with the doc so I knew ..."

The doctor said, "This is the father of Lawrence Bond."

"Well, Pop, don't you worry about a thing. I'll ..."

I grabbed his shoulder and jerked him to his feet. "My name is Marty Bond and if I catch you dogging this job I'll break your back! Marty Bond—name mean anything to you?"

"Yes ... sir," he said weakly. "I know all about you."

I let go of him. "All right. Sorry I blew my cap, buddy. But it's not impossible they may try to finish him off."

"No one gets by this door, Mr. Bond."

"All right. Keep awake."

Outside the sky was red, and it was the start of one more muggy day. I had a dry, rotten taste in my mouth, but I felt at peace with the world, almost happy. If my hunch was cooking, my work was cut out for me and it was more than even money I'd end up with a bullet fired by a joker who couldn't care less if he killed me. No paralyzed hands for him, no fear. Old Marty, the gutless wonder, finally found his out.

I had a cup of java and a roll. It was a few minutes

after six. Bill Ash wouldn't be on yet, but the wholesale markets were already working a half a day. I headed for the Lande Meat Company, Inc.

It wasn't much to look at. The door was locked and the windows were painted black halfway up, with the name Lande Meat Company, Inc. lettered in with gold. The door was locked but Mr. Lande didn't even bother with a burglar-alarm system.

Looking over the top of the painted windows, I saw a couple of meat blocks, a partitioned office, and two big icebox rooms made of unpainted pine boards. There were a few other tables and some empty wooden crates piled at one end of the store.

There was a garage down the street and I dropped in there, asked one of the mechanics, "You know the guy who used to be the driver for the meat company on the corner?"

"Lou? Yeah, I know Lou. He in a jam?"

"No. Understand he ain't working for the meat outfit now. You know where he lives?"

"Lou's working—helping out at the Bay Meat." He measured me with his eyes. "Lou in trouble?"

"Lou ain't in anything. What's your Lou's last name?"

"Lou Franconi, what you think?"

He told me where the Bay Meat was and I walked along Front Street, watching the gangs of longshoremen waiting around the docks for the shape-up. I turned off and the Bay Meat Company was like Lande's—a large store—only there was a lot of action going on. Two small delivery trucks were backed up and men in white butcher coats and caps or paper hats were loading one truck and unloading the other. I went in.

Two men were cutting meat on chopping blocks, while crates of dead chickens were stacked high and dripping with melting ice. Legs of lamb were hanging from wall hooks. There was a bloody hunk of some kind of meat on a scale that hung from the ceiling, and through a window in a room-size icebox I saw another butcher making mountains of chopped meat at a grinder. A hatchet-faced joker left one of the blocks, a big knife still in his mitt, and asked in a Swedish accent, "Yeah, mister?"

"Lou Franconi around?"

"He's in the market. Should be back in a few minutes."

"I'll wait."

He didn't ask me who I was, merely went back to work. I found a chair and sat. They evidently supplied bars and restaurants, and there were a number of large wicker baskets against one wall, each with a bar or eating place tagged on the handle. The butchers were filling orders—hatchet-face weighed up a steak, wrapped it and tossed it into one of the baskets, and checked it off on an order pad. Then he went into the icebox and came out with a whole liverwurst, a bag of franks, and chopped meat.

In the other baskets I could see tins of frozen livers, turkeys, loins of pork, and other meats. There were three phones and they seemed to be working all the time. There was a kind of office at one end of the store, and some old guy who looked like a bookkeeper would answer a phone and then call out, "August—Palm Bar wants a fresh ham. How much?"

The butcher working with hatchet-face yelled back, "A buck ten a pound."

The bookkeeper told the guy on the other end of the phone and there was a sort of argument and the book-keeper put the phone down and called out, "August—talk to Palm."

August dropped a cleaver and picked up one of the phones, said, "Charlie? Yeah, yeah, that's right a buck ten a pound. So what you fighting with me for? Pork is sky-high on the market. Don't buy no hams. Look, we got some canned picnics from Holland you can have for ninety cents a pound. What? Charlie, you want ham or not? I'm busy. Okay, okay, they run about twelve pounds. What else you want? How much chopped meat? Sure it's all lean, you know us."

Next to the icebox there was another room-sized wooden box without a window that must have been a deep-freeze—every few minutes one of the butchers would dash in and a foggy ice vapor would come out. Soon as he opened the door a light went on and I saw shelves with frozen turkeys, chickens, and meats—everything wrapped in some kind of plastic bags.

I was sitting there about ten minutes—August had been called to the phone twice and was bawling out the bookkeeper with: "How am I going to get the orders out if you keep me on the phone? Don't take no crap from them, tell 'em the price and they either take it or leave it"—when a stocky young guy breezed in carrying a half a cow, or something, on his shoulder. He was wearing a white butcher coat but no hat and he had thick bushy hair. He hung the meat on a hook, and hatchet-puss jerked his thumb at me and the guy came over, asked, "Looking for me, mister?"

"Want to talk to you."

"Cop?"

I nodded. "Any other cops been around to see you, Lou, today?"

"Today has just started. What's the matter? I only got two tickets in the last months and I paid... There was a young cop talked to me a couple of days ago. Called me and said he was going to drop in yesterday."

"Drop in where?"

"Here. Said he'd be around at closing time. Never

showed. What's up?"

"That young cop was beaten up yesterday afternoon, hurt bad."

"That's tough. How did it happen? I ... Hey, you ain't tying me in with anything like that?"

"All I want is a couple of answers, mainly about your ex-boss Lande."

Franconi grinned. "Willie ain't my ex-boss, I'm still working for him, and if you think Willie did it, you're way up the wrong tree. He's jerky but not tough."

"I didn't say Wilhelm—Willie—did anything or that he's connected with the beating. Matter of fact this isn't an official visit, sort of off the cuff."

"Hey, that's what the other cop told me. He wasn't a real copper, was he?"

"He was real enough. Let me ask the questions."

"Sure. You, you got copper written all over you?'

"Did anybody else know the young cop was to meet you here yesterday?"

Franconi shook his head. "No. I didn't tell nobody, didn't think much of it."

"Think about it now: sure there wasn't a single other person you mentioned it to?"

"Naw. He called and said he wanted to see me and I says I knock off here at five and he says he'll be here. I'll give it to you straight—I forgot all about it till yesterday. I was halfway up the street on my way home when it come to me. I came back here and waited for about ten minutes and he never showed. Naw, I know I didn't tell nobody because like I say I never thought nothing of it—like this cop was some kind of boy scout or something."

"Anybody else call you yesterday, stop you on the street?"

"Just my wife. She calls me every day and I pick her

up on the way home. I kid her about it, you know, a pickup every day." Lou grinned like a kid.

"What did you mean by Willie Lande not being your ex-boss? Still working for him?"

"I sure am, just picking up some extra greens here. Tell you, I think Willie is headed for the bughouse. Started acting nuts about a month ago."

"What means nuts?"

"See, Willie is a small-time outfit, I mean smaller than this one. He's the butcher, does all the buying and making up orders, hustles up sales. Me, I deliver the stuff. Job isn't bad, sixty-five a week take-home pay, but no loafing. I'm in the market early in the morning with Willie to pick up the meat, then I help him fill orders, and spend the afternoon delivering while Willie is out hunting up business. Sometimes I make two deliveries a day, so I got to keep going at high speed. This meat deal is a rat race."

"Just the two of you working there, no bookkeeper, or nobody?"

Franconi nodded. "Except during Christmas when he'd hire a school kid to help me, and his wife would come down to help with the phone calls." He lowered his voice. "Union would have my rear if they knew, but I help out by making the chopped meat, clean turkeys, fill what orders I can. Like I say, it's hard work but the pay is okay and Willie don't mind if I take home meat every day. With prices the way they are, that's a savings you ..."

"What did you mean when you said this was a rat race?"

Franconi took a deep breath, rattled off, "In this racket there's two things you got to watch: one that the bar or restaurant don't fold owing you a bundle, because some of them go out like flies—the overhead is big, you understand. The other things is—watch out a rival don't take your customers. Take Willie, for example; on a new account he takes it easy the first few weeks, keeps his prices down so maybe he's only breaking even, even losing a few cents. Then he slowly raises them. If the restaurant is a sharpshooter, when he feels the wholesaler is trying to goose him, he switches to a new one. But he has to play it careful too—if he should miss a day's meat, for example, he'd be in a spot, maybe have to close up. In the meat business—in the food business— everybody is screwing the other guy—but not too hard."

"Lande doing much business?"

Franconi let out a sharp laugh, a bark. "That's a good question, mister. He *had* a fair business, good steady accounts. What he has now is anybody's guess, probably nothing. And the way he played it smart—the cook is the key man in these places, and Willie would treat them right—a turkey here, a couple of steaks any time they wanted them, bottles of rye on Christmas wrapped in ten-buck bills. This way, if the meat is grade C instead of A, or a little under the weight, they don't say nothing. And if a guy called up and needed anything in a hurry, I'd dash right over. A nice setup, so about three weeks ago Lande chucks it all."

"Why?"

Franconi shrugged. "Willie come down on a Monday and says his ticker did a double jump over the week end, and the doc told him to either take a rest or plan to live in a wooden box. You see the story now: his customers got to have meat, so they'll turn to a new butcher—Bay has a couple of them already—be fed low prices for a while. A week from now when Willie gets back in business, he'll have to start from scratch."

"Let me get this straight—Lande worked years to build up a set of customers, then threw them over like that?"

"That's the picture. I don't get it because if his ticker is bad he could have hired a butcher, and sat on his can. Okay, Willie wouldn't have made dough, but he would still have his customers. Of course he give me four weeks' salary so I can't kick."

"And he expects to open again in about a week?"

"That's what he told me—come back in a month."

"Did Lande act sick?"

"Look, boss, I ain't no doctor and in this business most of the owners act like nervous wrecks all the time, but about two months ago, maybe six weeks, I notice Willie is up in the air a lot. I can tell—he starts forgetting things, and cursing."

"Cursing? He call people sons of bitches, bastards?"

"Naw, he only has one curse, something in Dutch that means may your spit turn into stone. What you guys after him for, unpaid taxes?"

"Why, does he keep a double set of books?" I asked.

"Naw, at least not that I know, and I know about everything in the business. He's like all the rest: he'll shortweight you and maybe slip in some poor-grade meat, but I can't picture Willie doing anything real crooked. He's just another hard-working slob, a little tight with the buck—that's why I near dropped dead when he hands out four weeks' salary like that. Jeez, I paid off my TV set."

"Anything doing at Lande's store while he's shut down? He seems to be down at the shop a lot."

"Naw. The market is like a fish bowl—everybody knows what's going on. I stick my head in every day when I go back to the old coffeepot for lunch. He isn't doing anything but cleaning up his books, trying to dun some of his bad accounts."

"Did you know Lande reported a stick-up a few days ago? Then denied it? Claimed two punks got him for fifty grand in his store."

Franconi stared at me like I was telling him a dirty joke, then burst into real laughter. "I never heard that, but fifty grand! Why Willie never saw more than five hundred bucks at any one time. Fifty grand—say, hey!"

"There's rumors his wife has a new mink and a car. Willie gamble?"

"He wouldn't bet a dime on tomorrow showing. Mister, you don't get him—he's one of these refugees, you know, work hard and no sense of humor. Funny thing, one of the other guys in the market mentioned seeing Bebe—that's his wife—driving a Caddy. I thought it was just a lot of hot air. Maybe it belongs to a friend or something."

"Lande have anyplace he might get a bundle of dough from? Any rich relatives or friends, or did he collect an insurance policy lately?"

"You got me there. I don't know his pals, but he usually put in a sixteen-hour day so he didn't have much chance to sport it up. Think he once told me he had some cousins in this country, but most of his people were bombed out in the war. He ain't no spender or ..."

Hatchet-face came over and said, "Lou, run over to Rosey's and pick up a hundred pounds of pull-its, and watch out for his scale."

I stood up, walked him out to his panel truck. "Thanks, Lou, and keep this under your hair. Willie is nervous and nothing may come of all this, no sense getting him excited."

"Mister, I ain't the talkative type. Anything else you want to know? Don't pay no attention to him," he jerked his thumb back toward the store, "I ain't breaking my ass for them."

"That's about all, wanted to get a general idea of the business. You know how it is, we have to look into all the corners."

"I know, I been to the movies," he said, winking. "Mister, I'm not one to tell you your job, but Lande wouldn't do nothing real crooked. Plenty of times I had a chance to buy us some hot meat, but he was too scared."

"That's why I want you to keep things quiet—all this may be a waste of time. Lou, one more thing, can you get me a list of the restaurants, bars, night clubs, Willie sold to? All the customers he'd had this last six months or so?"

"Easy, only about twenty-five of 'em. I delivered to them every day. Hold still, I'll write them out." He reached into the truck and took out a piece of wrapping paper, started writing.

When he gave me the list I thanked him, told him again to keep his trap shut, and maybe I'd drop in to see him again sometime.

"Glad to work with you—only don't get me in no trouble."

"Can you get into trouble, Lou—got a record?"

He shook his head too quickly. "No, sir. That is, nothing but a lot of traffic tickets ... expect that when you're delivering and ... yeah, I once did thirty days on the island for disorderly conduct. Kid gang stuff."

"All right, don't worry and just keep working with me. See you."

I started for the precinct, and the day was already so hot the heat waves were making me dizzy. I stopped at a couple of bars, not for beers, but to relieve my gut— my lousy tumor was really acting up.

It was just before nine when I reached the police station and Ash wasn't in yet. The desk sergeant was an old-timer whose face I remembered. He told me, "The lieutenant is a busy beaver these days, Bond. We're trying to check where the hell Cocky Anderson was before he died and it seems he dropped completely out of sight for at least a week before he ate lead. Want to see the lieutenant about anything special?"

"I'll drop back. When do you expect him?"

"Now, this afternoon, any time. Downtown is putting the screws on. You know these big cases, somebody will be the patsy if they don't come up with the killer pronto, so Bill—the lieutenant—is rushing around like he swallowed a firecracker."

"I'll be back sometime this morning. Tell him to wait for me," I said and walked out.

I didn't know how to kill an hour or so. I could go back to the Grover and catch some shut-eye, but I'd certainly have a run-in with King and that nance Lawson, and I didn't want to be bothered with petty arguments this morning.

I had some orange juice and a plate of French fries, and went down to the Lande Meat Company, Inc. The door was slightly ajar and I walked in. There was nobody around, but after a couple of minutes a little guy wearing a sweater under a white butcher coat, and an old homburg atop his thick face, stepped out of the icebox room and almost jumped through the ceiling when he saw me. He said, "Got the wrong store. I'm not open." He spoke with a slight accent.

"I got the right store, Lande."

"What is this—what you guys want?"

"What guys?"

"You don't fool me, you're a cop. You want a salami sandwich?"

"Too hot for salami—I want to talk to you."

"I'm a sick man, an honest businessman taking inventory. I ain't parked by a hydrant or nothing, I give to the PAL—let me alone." He had a fast way of talking, skipping from phrase to phrase.

"Where did you get the fifty grand from?"

He smacked himself on the chest. "Me? Do I look like a man with fifty thousand dollars?"

"Bebe bought a mink recently, a Caddy—she didn't get them with soap coupons."

"You got no right to ask me questions—I didn't do nothing," he said, going to the other end of the store and taking a handful of sawdust out of a barrel. "We had some dollars in a safe-deposit vault. When I got a stroke a few weeks ago, I tell the wife, What we keeping this for? We can't take it with us, let's spend it."

He spread the sawdust on a wooden chopping block, then took a steel brush from the wall, started scraping the block top.

"Willie, those two kids who were bumped off over in New Jersey—one of them talked in the hospital before he died, said he'd stuck you up for fifty grand." It was a clumsy lie and he didn't tumble, kept cleaning the block, both hands on the brush.

"We're passing this on to the income-tax boys—they're interested."

"Interested in what? Let anybody find an income of fifty thousand for me and I'll be glad to pay—give them half."

"Lande, maybe you don't know how the tax boys work once they bite into a case. All right, maybe they can't find no record of the cash, but they watch you. Maybe five years from now you think it's safe to take the dough out of your mattress. The second you buy a house, a car, take a cruise, they crack down on you like white on rice, asking where you got the dough from."

I could have been talking to myself. Lande put the brush away, waved the tails of his coat over the block to brush off any remaining sawdust.

"Willie, the young cop you first reported the robbery to, he was almost killed yesterday."

He jumped at that, paled, fought to get control of himself. He went into the icebox and came out with a liverwurst. He sliced off a piece, began eating it—nearly choking on it.

I walked over and he put the knife down, motioned for me to cut myself a hunk. I slapped him on one fat cheek, knocking him halfway across the store. A loud stinging slap will scare a joker more than a solid punch that might put him away. Get slapped right and you think they've pulled the world down around your ears.

"Willie, this ain't a picnic, a time for sandwiches and ..."

Lande let out a shrill scream of fear. I'd made a mistake; I'd knocked him near the door and he turned over, got to his feet, ran outside. It seemed only a second later when he returned with two cops, yelling, "Get that—him—out of here!"

Through the open door I saw a radio car at the curb as one of the cops gripped his night stick, asked, "What you doing in here, Mac?"

"Slicing liverwurst with Lande."

"He's a cop and he threatened me, punched me!" Willie shrilled; he was on full steam, ready to explode.

"Got a shield?" one of the cops asked me.

I didn't answer.

The other cop said, "Impersonating a policeman, that's a ..."

They were both young cops, probably on the force less than half a dozen years. I said, "Get the hay out of your ears, boys. I'm an ex-cop, retired. I never told Willie I was a cop. Ask him if I ever said I was a cop. Come on, Willie, tell them you don't want no trouble because you and I know it might be *big* trouble, awful *big*."

Lande swayed on his feet, face flushed, trying to think—think hard. He sort of gasped, "Yah, we were kidding around over a hunk of liverwurst, then he hit me."

"Just slapped him," I added,

"I think he's drunk," Willie said.

"Did he claim he was a cop?"

"I ain't making no charges," Willie said quickly. "Please, all I want is for him to get out of here, leave me alone!"

"Did he say he was a cop?"

"Tell him I never said nothing," I said.

One of the cops turned to me. "Close your kisser, let him talk."

"No, he never ... said ... no," Lande said.

The first cop turned to me. "What's your name?"

"Marty Bond." I didn't make the mistake of reaching for my wallet to prove it. I could see the cop trying to recall where he'd heard the name before. Then he asked, "That tin-badge cop they sapped up yesterday—that your boy?"

I nodded.

He motioned to his partner and they had a whispered conference for a moment as Willie wailed, "Cops, cops, all I get in my store is ..."

"Now take it slow," the cop said. "Where's your phone?"

Lande nodded at his office. One cop called in while the other leaned against the door, wiped his sweaty face with his free hand. Willie whispered to me. "Please, mister, leave me alone! I'm a sick man! I don't know what you want ... but leave me alone!"

"That's right, Willie, all this might give you another stroke —or a bullet in your back."

The flush in his face got deeper, then sheet-white as he grabbed at the meat block and crumpled to the floor. The cop at the door said, "Heat's got him!" and started for the sink. He stopped, told me, "You! Go over and get him a glass of water."

He was a smart cop.

I got a glass of water and let Lande have it on the puss. The other cop came out of the office as Willie opened his eyes, shook his head like a groggy fighter. The cop asked, "Want to go to the hospital?"

Lande sat up, struggled to his feet. "No. No. I'll see my own doctor. I have these attacks and ..."

I asked, "Who's your doctor?"

"Shut up!" the smart cop told me. He turned to Willie. "Sure you feel okay?"

"Yah, yah. I'm fine. I'll go home now and rest." Willie looked around. "You boys want some liverwurst?"

"No wonder you passed out—that stuff will kayo you in this heat," the cop who phoned said. He jerked his thumb at me. "Come on, Lieutenant Ash wants to see you at the station house."

"You mean you're taking me in?"

"Cut the clowning, Bond. You're not under arrest—I only have orders to bring you in."

"I suppose it beats walking."

The three of us went out to the radio car and I looked back and Wilhelm wasn't in the doorway—I wondered who he was phoning.

One of the cops got behind the wheel, then I got in, and the other cop turned his gun belt around so it wasn't next to me, and squeezed in. He was pretty good, only forgot one thing—he should have frisked me.

It was a short ride to the station house and nobody talked. The desk officer motioned toward the stairs and when one of the radio cops started walking back with me, the desk said, "That's all, get back to your car."

Bill looked like he'd missed a lot of sleep and for the first time since I'd known him he was wearing a dirty shirt. I sat down as he shut the door, and walking back to his desk he asked, "For the love of tears, Marty, you gone nuts?"

"Forget me—for a moment. I been trying to see you. What are you doing about Lawrence besides sticking a guard outside the hospital room?"

"We're getting these volunteer cops out, stupid ever having them here. I told them ..."

"Forget the volunteer cops, what about Lawrence?"

"I have a detective out checking on his friends. Usual routine."

"That all?"

"That all? What do you expect me to do, Marty? Put out a dragnet because some drunk or an old buddy of the kid's finally catches up with him? I got troubles with my own kid—Margie says she had a hundred and four fever all night. Lousy doctors, when they don't know what it is it becomes a 'virus.' And on this goddam Anderson mess, I'm running into enough blank walls to build a damn house."

"Things sure have changed—when I was on the force if a cop in uniform was slugged we'd turn the town upside down. No matter whether he was wearing a phony uniform or not, whoever slugged the kid *thought* he was a cop. I bet you haven't even questioned the boy yet."

"The docs said he couldn't be talked to till this afternoon. Marty, I been up all night, out with five men, checking on Cocky Anderson's pals. Marty, Marty, I know he's your son—stepson—but for the love of tears don't make a big thing out of this. What do you expect me to do?"

"I want you to forget Cocky Anderson for a few minutes and listen to me. I talked to Lawrence early this
morning. Somebody called him into a hallway and ..."

"Hell, I know the details. It's one of those ritzy small
apartment houses—most of the people were out. Nobody heard anything, saw anything, till an ad man who
lives on the third floor came home and found the kid.
We've checked the tenants; none of them knew the kid.
They're all big shots, not the criminal type."

"While you're checking, look right around here. Somebody in this station house must have tipped off whoever
did it that Lawrence was coming in for some extra patrol
work."

"Maybe the kid was followed, maybe it was one of
those things where the guy happened to see him and let
him have it. Marty, these CD cops have their own setup.
The guy in charge here is some retired West Pointer, a
big society buddy—he wouldn't have any part in a beating. Don't start turning my precinct on its head with a
lot of wild ideas."

"I got some wilder ones. Listen to me: all Lawrence
remembers is dimly seeing a guy that looked like Dick
Tracy and ..."

"Dick Tracy? For the love of ...!"

"Bill, listen. I think that Dick Tracy stuff is a good
make. He also heard the guy cursing him before he
blacked out. The guy kept saying, 'Bastid! Bastid'—like
a growl. I think it was Bob 'Hilly' Smith!"

Ash stood up, kicked the table. "Between the brass,
the reporters and you, I'll be ready for a strait jacket!
Why would a top operator like Smith go around slugging
a tin cop?"

"I don't know the why, for now, only that there's a lot
of loose ends to this thing. The kid was worked over by
a professional, and Bob is the best in the business. Re-

member what Bob was known as before he became so big? 'Pretty Boy' Smith they called him. He has those overclean-cut features, the strong face of a Dick Tracy. Finally, he came up from the tobacco road, a mountain boy, and don't talk so good. I remember his favorite word was *bastid*. Never *bastard* but *bastid*."

"Damn it, Marty, all the booze you've lapped up has softened what few brains you ever had," Bill said, his voice snotty, like he was talking to a lunkhead. "There's a million so-called clean-cut-looking punks. There's also about four million people in Brooklyn alone who use the word *bastid*. As for it being a professional going-over, that's bunk. A maniac can do a better job than any paid hood."

"No, he can't—and remember me, I'm an authority on how to beat up a guy. All right, a nut may kill faster than a professional, but this wasn't a killing—this was a beating, a warning. The doc at the hospital says Lawrence was beaten in a matter of seconds; the guy didn't waste a blow—that's a pro muscleman. Maybe it's wacky, but I think the kid stepped into something with this nutty butcher, something big enough to make a Bob Smith scare him off. This Wilhelm Lande is phony, he never had a stroke—or he would have had one just now. And he's scared, real scared."

Ash walked around the tiny drab room. His pants were wrinkled, his shoes unshined. "Marty, hold up a minute, don't go off the deep end on this. I like the kid too, I'm not sloughing this off. But think what you're saying—Hilly Smith is the top syndicate cop. Even if he wanted to slug a CD rookie, he wouldn't do it himself. And he isn't walking the streets. We've been looking for him, routine pickup on Anderson, and Smith can't be found. As for that butcher mess, Marty, do you realize what you're saying? For the love of tears the guy wasn't

robbed to start with—there's no charge—and now you
want me to believe a lousy little butcher hired the best
muscleman in the rackets to beat up an auxiliary police
kid who was horsing around with a robbery that never
was!"

I shrugged. "All right, I'm not saying this is the blue-
print, and I know it's a wild hair, but I think it's worth
looking into. Or is Bob Smith so big and protected
you're afraid to touch him on a minor case?"

"Cut that kind of wind. There's nothing I'd like better
than to get that muscle rat—on anything. Marty, you
know me, I'm no hero but I never side-stepped anything
because of the angles. I got a man working on Lawrence's
case, and with this Anderson thing all over town, it's
hard to spare a man. What you forget is there can be a
hundred reasons why the kid was slugged—a drunk, a
cop-hater, a nut, and maybe something in the kid's back-
ground neither of us know about."

"Don't cover me with it, Bill, it's up to my shoes now."

He stopped walking and came over to me. "What
makes you so all fire sure, Marty? This is the first time
you've seen Lawrence in ten years, maybe longer. You
don't know a damn thing about him. I think he's a good
kid and I'm not saying he's mixed up in anything, you
understand. But neither am I dropping everything and
buying a crazy yarn about a two-bit butcher and a top
racket man being interested in beating up a cop-happy
kid, who wasn't on duty, wasn't even empowered to act
as a peace officer. He was just an ordinary citizen who
got into a fight, and because I happen to know the kid,
I'm doing more than I should to find who walloped
him!"

I got up. "So long, Bill."

"I got more to tell you, Marty. Close the door for a
second." I shut the door, leaned against it, my stomach

rumbling. Ash glanced down at his dirty shirt, as if realizing for the first time that he'd been up all night. Then
he looked at me and tried to smile as he said, "Marty,
this is tough to say because in our own way we've been
pals for a long time. I know you got a lousy temper, fly
off the handle. Maybe your toughness was a kite and I
was the tail when you were flying high. Marty, I try
never to kid myself. I know I've been lucky and therefore
..."

"Too hot for a speech—what you want to say, Bill?"

"Just that you're no longer a cop, Marty. You can't go
busting into people's places, question them—slap them
around. In short, you can't take the law into your own
hands. It wasn't exactly legal when you had a badge—
now you haven't any badge. You have a burr up your
prat about the kid, I understand that, but ... Hell, Marty,
for your own good I'm telling you this in front—don't
make me run you in; this is my precinct and I'm dancing
on enough hot coals now—if I catch you playing cop
again, I'll have to throw you in the can."

"The gold on your badge is making your eyes blood-
shot, Bill. There's an angle you don't know here. This
means a lot more to me than getting hunk for a badge-
happy kid, especially if it is Hilly Smith. You and me,
we've made a lot of collars, some good scores, but always
the two-bit punks, the small-time hustlers, the little op-
erators. For once I want to nail down a big boy, a top
apple. Maybe to make up for all the slobs I've pushed
around."

Ash stared at me, then his tight face relaxed and he
burst out laughing. "This is a new one—never thought
I'd see the day your conscience would be bothering
you—I thought it was made of pig-iron. Marty, I'm not
being the big cop with you because I like the idea, but I
haven't time for anything till this Anderson deal is ..."

"Cocky's death is just another headline to me, another dead crook."

Bill sighed. "Okay, Marty, Cocky's death is my job and I got to get back to it. But remember, I'm warning you to stop playing cop."

"Let's both of us play this warning game. Keep out of my way, Bill, or you'll get hurt." I walked out of his office. Downstairs I stopped at the desk, asked, "Where's the guy in charge of the auxiliary police unit here?"

"Colonel Flatts is downtown, arranging about the transfer of his men out of here."

"Flatts—what's his first name?"

"F. Frank Flatts. All f's—his mother must have had that on her mind."

I went out into the morning heat, got a couple of packages of mints and an ice-cream soda, took a bus downtown to the license bureau. I was lucky—one of the old-timers I knew hadn't gone out to lunch yet and I took him out for a fat sandwich and a couple of beers, listened to the details of his wife's fallen womb, gave him the list of Lande's customers, and told him I would call later to get the names of the real owners.

Then I taxied up to a couple of gin mills off Broadway, asked around for two good stoolies I used to own. But "used to" was a half a dozen years ago and they'd disappeared. Then I called a detective in the midtown area to have him check on Lou Franconi's record—only to find the sonofabitch had retired four months before.

I phoned Dot, asked, "Where can I find this girl Lawrence was running around with?"

"She works in the office of a lawyer named Lampkin, near Chambers Street. Why do you want to see her?" There was more life in Dot's voice.

"Routine stuff, can't overlook anything—the trouble is there should be six of me to handle all the details.

You been to the hospital this morning?"

"I called. Lawrence is sleeping comfortably, went to sleep as soon as he talked to you, the doctor said. Marty, I was a little hysterical last night, but I really appreciate this."

"All right. As usual I have my own reasons for looking into this. Dot, was the kid mixed up in anything? I know he isn't the type, but with kids these days ... He wasn't in any gangs, stuff like that?" It was a wasted question to ask a mother.

"Of course not. And Lawrence isn't a kid—he's a man."

"You bet. Look, what's the name of his babe?"

"Helen Samuels."

"Can't you talk him out of marrying a Jew-girl, Dot?"

I heard her sigh over the phone. "Marty, will you ever grow up?"

"Honey, I'm way past the growing stage. Maybe I'll see you at the hospital."

I took the subway down to Chambers Street, looked up this Lampkin in the phone book. He shared a suite of offices with a football team of other lawyers. A pretty, big-eyed girl, with a solid bosom, was at the reception desk. When she asked what I wanted, I said, "Are you Helen Samuels?"

"Yes." Her eyes got that wary look most citizens get when anybody "official looking" asks for them.

"I'm Marty Bond, Lawrence's stepfather."

"He's talked about you often."

"Can we chatter for a couple of minutes? Here? Or will it get you in a jam?"

"We can talk here. I just called the hospital. Larry is much better."

"Look, Helen, you know about me—I'm an ex-cop. I'm on my own and trying to find who beat up Lawrence.

I have to narrow down any and all leads, so I'm going to ask you a couple of questions that may sound silly, but give me the truth."

"I understand. What do you wish to know, Mr. Bond?"

"How long have you known Lawrence?"

"Oh—about three years. We met in college."

"I take it you know him sleeping well. Was he mixed up in anything shady? And before you shout no at me, think. A lot of kids try dope for a kick these days, find themselves in a swindle."

"Larry was not in anything like that, I'm utterly positive."

"All right, utterly. Did he do any gambling?"

"Of course not. Sometimes we played bridge for a half a cent a hundred, or penny poker, that's all."

"Where'd he get all his money from?"

"What money? Why, we were using my salary.... Oh, that's a trick question, isn't it?"

"A clumsy one. You have any other boy friends, jealous ones?"

"No. I haven't dated anyone but Larry since we met."

"Lawrence wanted—wants—to be a lawyer. Was he mixed up in politics, hanging around any of the clubs?"

"Never. You see he didn't plan on practicing law; he expects to be a policeman."

"You like that idea?"

She shook her head, a big shake that made her breast-works dance. I wondered if Lawrence was man enough to handle all that. "No, I didn't, not at first. But then when I understood how much law and law enforcement mean to him, I wanted him to become a police officer."

"Believe me, he'll be better off as a lawyer. There's a difference of religion—your parents object to Lawrence?"

"Not after they met him. And I haven't any brothers

who hated Larry either!"

"All right, don't get ahead of me. I have to ask these questions. Is there anybody, for any reason you know of, who might have hated Lawrence? Maybe another CD cop, maybe a guy in college—anybody who even disliked him?"

"No, nobody."

"Thanks, you've been a help. Good-by."

"Well, I've told you the truth, answered ..."

"I know, and I mean it—about your being a big help. Thanks."

Outside I stopped for a glass of iced coffee, tried to re-member the name of the CD cop Lawrence had been teamed with when Lande said he was robbed. My mem-ory was still good and it came to me—John Breet. I looked in all the phone books—no Breets.

Long as I was downtown I dropped in to see the joker at the license bureau. He had the list of owners, but far as I knew none of them were racket people.

I went into a bar and used their bathroom, had a ham-burger. Maybe I was rusty, being away from the job all these years, but I felt like an amateur. Bill was right, I was spouting off about Hilly Smith like a comic-book dick. If Bob was in this, there had to be a tie-up between the kid and the syndicate, or Lande and the crime mob. The kid seemed clean, and what the hell would the syn-dicate care about a two-bit butcher? Lande could be a numbers drop, but the driver would have hinted at that—unless he was in on the deal too. But that didn't add up, the store was too isolated; the longshoremen played their numbers right on the docks. Still there had to be some connection, or Smith was out—and so was the little favor I planned on his doing for me.

I found F. Frank Flatts in the phone book, in the ritzy part of the East Side. I took a gamble and sweated out a subway ride up there. The colonel lived in an apartment house with a doorman and a guy with a death mask for a puss who operated a switchboard. Flatts was in, and when I explained I was Lawrence's father, he had me up.

He looked like a real character, brushed gray hair, wearing a heavy smoking robe and slippers, nose and lips like knives, and he walked and stood like he'd swallowed a broomstick—the erect military posture, or something. He was a guy with dough; he even had a butler.

Of course he had to speak with a clipped, society accent, biting off and freezing each word. He said, "My dear man, I can't tell you how upset I am about what happened and I assure you I'm doing everything possible to find the culprits." His eyes took in my sweaty shirt, my baggy clothes.

"Look, Colonel, save the oil. I'm a former army officer myself...."

"Regular army, sir?"

"Nope, just a clown who lumbered through OCS. Also, I'm an ex-cop, retired."

"Then you certainly understand how disturbed I was at ..."

"Colonel, let me tell you why I'm here. When I was on the force I was a hot-shot detective. Well, today I've found out it's rugged working on your own. In the old days, while I was hunting down a lead, the department would have a dozen other men running down minor clues. That's what I'm up against now; I can't do this alone."

"You have my complete co-operation, and I think your civic pride is to be commended."

"That's what I want—your co-operation, your influence. The cops are busy now, won't work with me. I figure you can put a little pressure on them, get them to find out a few facts for me. I want some records checked; for example, I want to know more about one of your men, a John Breet, who was with Lawrence the night ..."

"My dear sir, there is no need to question any of my men—they have all been screened before joining the force. As for the police, I am sorry to say they have not co-operated with us, nor appreciated our efforts in the least. I am not talking about any particular police officer, but the department as a whole. They seem to think we are a kind of joke, a stumbling block, underestimating our effectiveness."

"Colonel, there's a big murder hunt on at the moment—the heat is on the force. In fact the heat is on pretty much all the time—they haven't the time to work with your men. But that's not what I'm here for. I take it you're wealthy, have influence, not to mention your position in CD. What I want you to do is pull strings, insist somebody in the department work with you—then you can get me the dope I need."

He shook his head. "Mr. Bond, I assure you that we, as an auxiliary police force, are doing everything we can to solve this beating. Also, I am sure that the regular police force isn't ..."

"Colonel, you just said you'd give me full co-operation. Well, that's what I'm asking for."

"I will in any official capacity. As for pulling ... strings, using special influence, favoritism, I have always been against that. I will do everything I can—through channels."

"Through channels? Are you for real? This has to be taken care of now, today, tomorrow, or it never will be solved."

"As a former officer you must see my position. I can't ..."

"I don't see no position—I ain't playing checkers. All

I'm asking you to do is make a few calls for me. Won't take you more than a couple of hours, and with the information I'll be able to hook up, or throw out, a lot of loose ends in the case. Will you do that?"

"If you tell me what you want, I will suggest it to the police department, and to my own ..."

"Flatts, do you know the police commissioner, or know anybody who knows him?"

"As it happens, I know the commissioner quite well. I also know the mayor, but I fail to see ..."

"Will you call the commissioner right now, tell him to put you in touch with a detective who will work with you?"

"I see no reason for ..."

I headed for the door. "Colonel, those eagles on your shoulders must have dropped something—your head."

He was starting to draw himself up as I left.

There was one check that would take a lot of phoning, so I went back down to the Grover. Dewey was on, said, "King left a message for you—unless you call him right away, you're through."

"I haven't time to worry about that underfed mouse. Any trouble last night?"

"One of Barbara's customers tried drinking in the lobby, but left after I talked to him. Don't know what's happened to Lilly; we've been short a maid now for the second day. Oh yeah, this Dr. Dupre was in, wants you to call him. Marty, see the doc—you must be sick, screwing up a good job like ..."

"Don't worry about me, Dewey. Give me an outside line in my room."

I undressed and took a sponge bath, then started calling guys I knew in the department. It took over an hour, and a lot of "Where you been all these years, Marty old boy?" before I found one who had an in with the Immigration Department. He gave me a name to call and I got my info in a few minutes—nothing. Lande's real name was Landenberg. He'd come to this country in the late 30's with his wife, and a relative in jersey City, a Herman Bochstein, a bricklayer turned building contractor, had stood bond for him.

That was that—I'd spent all day running in empty circles. I stretched out, but it was too hot for sleep. It was after four and I decided to go over to the hospital, see how Lawrence was, give him a talking to.

As I left, Dewey asked, "When will you be back?"

"I don't know."

"What shall I tell King if he calls?"

I told him what to tell King and went out. The streets were like an oven as I headed over toward Seventh Avenue. One of the maids, a big wide dark woman, was walking ahead of me, and as I passed she said, "Heat is a brute, isn't it, Mr. Bond? That Lilly, we got to work twice as hard with her out."

"It's tough all, over. Maybe she'll be back tomorrow."

"She don't—you'd better get an extra woman to fill in or you going to have me out."

She turned the corner and I hadn't walked more than a few hundred feet alone when I had this feeling I was being followed. I've never been wrong about a hunch—when it came to being tailed. Because of the heat, the streets were pretty empty; I did all the usual tricks, but I couldn't make my tail or throw him off. Finally I ducked down some subway steps, put a token in the turnstile. There were less than a dozen people along the uptown platform, and I kept watching the turnstiles. Nobody came through except an old dame—yet I knew I was being followed.

I jumped on the first train that came in—a Bronx express. I sat down, and all this rushing made me sweat—

wet. I was going to shake the tail by jumping off at Times Square, hop another train, or bluff it ... then I got a better idea. It was too hot for all that work—I'd take my tail for a little ride—up to Harlem.

Except for a few days, I'd never worked in Harlem and it was just as well—the place gave me the shakes. I felt like an open target: a burly white man in Harlem could only be a cop. I've known cops who said working Harlem was a good deal, but not me. I expected to be jumped any and every moment, was full of this uneasy fear.

I tried spotting my tail in the store windows—there weren't many whites walking around—but I couldn't make him. I hoped he was as nervous as me.

Lilly lived in a room in an old brownstone with about ten bells at the entrance. I rang her bell four times, like it said above her name, and before she could buzz back, the door opened and two big dark men came out, rough-looking jokers. The way they looked at me as I went in, I thought they were going to try and stop me, but they just went on out, down the steps.

I walked up two flights of stairs, full of the smells of too many people living in one place, wondered what the hell I was doing up here. It wasn't the money—I sure didn't need dough now—it was just the idea of being screwed, somebody putting something over on me.

Lilly's dark face was at a door opening, and from what little I could see of her, she was in a nightgown. She looked astonished when she saw me but didn't make no move to open the door. I said, "Hello, Lilly."

"What you doing up here, Mr. Bond?"

"Just dropped in to talk to you—but not in the hall-way."

"I'm in my bed clothes, not dressed to admit no men.

Don't the hotel believe I'm sick? Got a cold in my shoulder that's about killing me. When I come back I'll bring
a certificate from my lodge doctor and ..."

"Cut it, Lilly, you know why I'm up here. Where's my
dough?" I kept my voice down.

"What money, Mr. Bond?" she said, her voice loud in
the quiet of the house.

If her room faced the front, I might make my tail from
the window, although he didn't seem that sloppy. "Let
me inside and we'll talk it over."

"No, I'm not letting you in my room. You drunk
again, Mr. Bond?"

"Don't get fresh—drunk again."

"What you mean, fresh? I'm not feeling well, and
there's a draft here. What you want?"

"Look, Lilly, I did you a favor. I got that five bucks for
you from them drunks, and this is the way you pay me
back. Trouble with you people, try to be nice and ..."

"What you mean by *you* people? Aren't you people,
Mr. Bond, a human being?"

I was getting sore. "All right, cut the lip. You were going to put a buck in for me on 506, remember?"

"Yes, I remember."

"Number 605 came out that day."

"So?"

"Lilly," I said, fighting to keep my voice low, "nobody
plays a number straight. You combinated the number—
means I had about fifteen cents of the buck on 605—I
want my seventy-five bucks."

"You must be drunk! I play 506 straight, always. And
if you'd won I'd have brought you your money, even if
I had to leave my sickbed."

"Lilly, don't play me for a sucker. I don't want no
trouble but ..."

"I'm catching cold talking to you?" She started to shut

the door and I stuck my foot in.

She stared at me, said evenly, "Mr. Bond, get your foot out of my door. This isn't the Grover; you ain't no kingpin up here."

"Keep your voice down! I ..."

"You don't scare me, you lout! When you dig a grave for me—dig two—one for yourself!"

For a moment I was so frightened I couldn't talk, then I asked, "Lilly, what made you say that—dig a grave for myself? You see something on my face? Or ... Tell me, Lilly, forget the dough and tell me why you said that. Dig a grave. I ..."

I took my foot out of the doorway and she slammed the door shut. For a moment the house was terribly still, then I heard other doors opening slowly, whispers. I looked around. From the floor above, a dark-faced little girl was staring down at me with frightened eyes.

I turned and walked down the torn carpeted wooden steps, knowing people were watching and listening behind the closed doors. I reached the street in a hurry, started walking fast. By the time I reached Lenox Avenue I felt better, a little sore at myself for being frightened. Hell, I'd smacked more than my share of black boys and never ...

At Lenox, like a chill wind, I got this feeling again about being tailed. I almost laughed. If my shadow was following me to see who I was working for—as he probably was—this trip to Harlem would sure puzzle the hell out of whoever he reported back to.

Anyway, maybe Lilly had played the number straight, and what difference did it make to me—money wouldn't buy nothing where I was going.

I rode the subway back down to Fourteenth Street. In St. Vincent's I phoned the police station, got Bill. "What's the idea of putting a tail on me?"

"A tail? Why should ...? Marty, will you leave me alone! Downtown just chewed my end out again. I haven't even thought of you."

"Don't bull me, I'm being followed."

"Then maybe Dick Tracy is tailing you!" Bill snapped, as he hung up.

Stepping out of the phone booth, I wiped the sweat from my puss with a damp handkerchief and grinned. Now that I was sure Bill didn't have a man on me, it was time I started carrying my gun. The fish were biting so good even a rusty old fisherman like me could land a shark ... the man-eating kind. Smith would be my sleeping pills, my ...

Dig a grave. Why would a sick old woman call me a lout?

Four

Whoever said youth is the best medicine had the right dope—it was remarkable how Lawrence had recovered from the beating in less than twenty-four hours. Of course he was still in bed, but his voice was good and they'd taken off some of the bandages on his face—I could see his blackened eyes, his lips and scrawny neck. The doc told me he hadn't found any more internal injuries and it would be at least a month before Lawrence would be able to walk out of the hospital.

As I saw the sparkle in his eyes when he saw me, and as I sat beside the bed and told him what I'd done, even my ideas about Bob Smith, I felt sorry for the boy. Maybe it was that skinny neck between all the bandages of his chin and chest. I decided once and for all I'd talk the kid out of his silly box-top ideas.

The boy listened without interrupting, finally said, "I

don't know, Marty. As you say, the big thing is the link, and what possible connection can there be between Lande and the top crime syndicate? Somehow, I agree with Lieutenant Ash—it doesn't make sense."

"Sure, it don't make a bit of sense—now. But it's something big, all right. I'm being tailed. That means soon as I left Lande this morning he got on the phone, yelled—to somebody. Somebody big because hiring a tail is an expensive deal."

The eyes nodded. "Be careful, Marty, although I know you can handle anything that comes along. I can't understand Ash's not working with you, but as you say he must be busy. Anything new on the Anderson killing?"

"Haven't had a chance to read a paper or hear the radio. Look, Lawrence, when you get out of here, I want you to promise me something—that you'll leave the auxiliary force and forget about taking the police exam."

Now his eyes actually blazed. "Why? Because I was ambushed you must think I'm not tough enough to be a real cop!" The words came out hard, almost curt.

"Lawrence, stop talking like you're a wide-eyed twelve-year-old. Know the true definition of 'tough'? It means you're scared. The tougher the joker, the more the coward. I found that out for the first time the other night—the hard way. So let's stop talking like children about being tough or brave—that's for the birds. I want you to forget trying to be a cop because you're an intelligent boy and you'll only break your heart. I tell you to forget it just as I'd tell you to forget any other lousy job."

"This is new—Marty the cop-hater!" he said, mocking me, his eyes sort of smiling at me above the bandages.

"I don't hate cops, it's only that we're called upon to do an impossible job. Kids rob because they're bored, thrill-happy, want a bang—but mostly because they're broke. So you stick them in jail and they come out broke, and other kids continue to be broke, and it goes on and on. What the hell real good do cops or laws do unless you change the cause of the lawbreaking?"

The cut lips parted in what passed for a smile, and his eyes became tender, like a gal's. "Marty, you astonish me—you have a social consciousness under that hard-boiled front."

"I haven't a social anything, but I've been around, seen the facts."

"I'm glad you have a sense of social welfare," Lawrence said. "And you're right—at best laws are only a salve for deeper social sores, but a salve is better than nothing. And until we reach an utopian era, I'll continue to love the law, try to see it is carried out and obeyed."

"You kidding? I told you the other night that not an hour goes by without mister average jerk citizen breaking a law—spitting on the sidewalk, sneaking a smoke in the subway, jaywalking. You can't enforce *all* the laws so right off the bat, because of a lack of time and men, a cop has to close his eyes to things ... and a cop with his eyes shut isn't a good cop. There is no such animal." Suddenly I didn't know why I was even talking to the silly kid. I felt tired, impatient with the dope—all band-aged up because he was a lousy tin hero and still arguing with me.

"You're wrong. You were a good cop," he said, "a real pro. And you still could be. You've been on my ... this beating ... less than a day and you've already nar-rowed it down to a point where you're ready for the break. That's efficient police work."

"Lawrence, kid, I'm a stumblebum. That's what I'm trying to tell you—I've been one all my life but never knew it till now. Let me give it to you straight, even if it won't be exactly pretty. I gather you think Bill Ash is what you call a 'good' cop?"

"I certainly do. I think he's capable, industrious, and steady."

"Let me show you something else he is, has to be. When I ... uh ... retired I needed a job and police work was the only thing I knew," I told him, talking slowly so he wouldn't miss a word, and because it was a little rough to put it in words. "I didn't have the connections for private jobs, the time and money to build up a clientele. I either had to be a guard in a bank, a walking gun, or luck up on something ... like being a hotel dick at the Grover. You've seen the joint; most hotels that size haven't a house man. You know what I really am there? I'm a combination bouncer and pimp. Yeah, p-i-m-p."

His eyes flashed surprise as he said, "Are you kidding? What are you telling me, Marty?"

"What is sometimes known as the truth, boy. We have from three to a dozen or more girls working there, with the money filtering up to one of the most respected real-estate outfits in town. All right, I had to take the job, as it was, or no job. Now let's get to Bill Ash. When we were partners we took our share of cushion, nothing big, a gift of a shirt or a hat here, a free supper or a bottle there—you come upon a stick-up and there's a lot of bills on the floor, you pocket a few, in a ..."

"Marty, I know cops are humans, and wear badges not halos."

"Kid, I'm trying to show you what a trap a cop's job is. The Grover is in Bill's precinct and was paying off the cops before he ever took over. Bill keeps a little hunk of the graft, the rest goes higher up. Here's your capable and decent Bill Ash—and he really is—who gets himself a fat promotion after twenty years of hard work. He knows the Grover is running a house—if he cracks down, the real-estate bigwigs with connections will have him booted out to the sticks before he can reach for his hat. Suppose Bill doesn't take the pay-off, merely shuts his eyes to things? All right, maybe he isn't being your 'good cop' then, but neither is he in the pimp business. But he can't even do that because the pimps would be jittery, never knowing when he would crack down. Of course he could bust the whole thing wide open, expose everybody from the police brass to the real-estate tycoons. In that case, I'd give odds that Bill would be framed, maybe even murdered."

The scorn in the boy's eyes almost cut me. He said, "My God, Marty, you're sick, crazy sick!"

"Not the way you think. I merely want to show you what you're getting into. Everybody hates a cop, the crooks and the so-called honest citizens. We all have some larceny in us, so at heart we're all anti-law. You're hated and pressured and overworked and underpaid, and no matter how honest you think you are, especially the big brass, you have to play politics in one form or another to keep the job—the graft machine is too well oiled to be stopped by a single cog."

He didn't say anything; his eyes searched the ceiling as if he didn't know I was there. Then he said, "How can you be so cynical, Marty? It sounds cheap coming from you, if you'll excuse my saying it. You, the most decorated cop on the force. I remember the time you rushed into a room with two gunmen waiting, and disarmed them. It gave me a kick to read the stories in the paper to the kids, tell them that was my dad. Tell me, why did you risk your life so often if what you say is true?"

I grinned, to hide a belch, my mouth filling with the lousy taste. "Lawrence, I did it partly because I was a fool, fell for the phony glory, my name in the paper, the jerks slapping me on the back. Maybe I was stupid-brave and maybe I wasn't such a brave joker—all the cards were marked in my favor. The average punk will rarely shoot a cop. In most cases it's when they don't know the ..."

"You forget my ... my father—shot down in uniform!"

I shook my head. "I said they rarely shoot, not that they never shoot. A rat will fight when he's cornered. Kid, in my book your dad was a fool. They had a gun in his back when he went for his own gun. Shooting him was almost a reflex action on the part of the hood. And according to regulations, your dad *had* to go for his gun. They expect you to risk your life when the odds are way against you—on what other job would you take that kind of crap? Jobs where you risk your life, normal risks, sandhog, steeplejack, high construction work, at least they pay you for the risk—here they reward you by letting you pay for your own bullets!"

"Marty, I wish you hadn't come here. I have to say this: you're old, slipping. No matter what you say, you put in many years, the best part of your life, in useful work as a cop. What's happened to you now, I don't know."

"Lawrence, care to hear about some of the 'useful' work I did as a cop?"

He shut his eyes. "No."

"Maybe it's what you need. Dot says I'm your ideal. Let me tell you about a few cases 'ideal' had. There's ..."

"I don't want to hear them."

"Lawrence, remember how interested you always were in any crime case? You'll like these. There's Mrs. De-Costa. I've ..."

"I'm not interested."

"Yes, you are," I said. "I've been dreaming about Mrs. DeCosta lately—nightmares. I don't know why. One night, at eleven-twenty, we get a call that three men are robbing a grocery store. Bill and I are due to go off duty at midnight, but we have to go over to the store. It

hadn't been entered but the door is partly jimmied. We
go across the street to this Mrs. DeCosta who phoned
in. She was living in the basement of a private house.
One of these stocky, healthy-looking blondes, about
thirty-five. She was wearing a bathrobe and I remember
all the nice creamy white skin of her shoulders.

"She says as she was getting ready for bed she glanced
across the street, saw three young guys trying to force
the door of the store. Says they ran as soon as our car
turned into the block. All right, by now it's almost midnight and I'm stuck on this lousy case. So I'm pretty
sore, in a rush. Dot was playing bridge, expected me to
call for her at ten after midnight—we didn't like to leave
you alone much. One of the troubles of being a cop,
never sure when you'll be off, can't make even ordinary
plans."

The kid still had his eyes closed and I wondered if he
was sleeping. Then he ran his tongue over his dry lips
and I knew he was listening. I told him, "I run out and
scout the block. On the corner I come on three wops,
although one of them turned out to be a Jew. All a little
juiced. In this business one rule you can go by is that
nine times out of ten the guy nearest the crime did it.
That's common sense. I flashed my badge, took the kids
back to the DeCosta apartment for her to identify them.
She says it was too dark to make out anybody's face
and she doesn't think it's these three because two of the
three she saw only had shirts on while all of these guys
are wearing jackets. Of course she has to blab this out
in front of them and they start smiling.

"By now it's near one and I'm getting no place. The
three ginzos of course deny everything, even though one
of them has a big screwdriver in his pocket that could
be used as a jimmy. Bill even pulls the roper line about
he's a witness, not a dick, keeps saying, 'That's them, all

right. I'm positive,' but the lice don't admit a thing. All right, three kids tried busting into a store, three kids are found within a block of the place. I bang them in the gut a couple of times—to scare them—when this De-Costa dame gets hysterical and shouts, 'What are you beating them for? I told you I can't identify them!'

"She's making a racket and from a curtained bedroom off the living room I'll be damned if a skinny colored guy in pajamas don't come limping into the living room, walking with canes. It turned out the guy was a spick, but to me they're all black, all dinges. He asks what's going on and the blonde says he's her husband. All right, maybe to your way of thinking it was none of my business, but I was tired and sore, and she had all that nice white bosom.... You see the way things add up, work out? I ain't got time to sit down, work by the book, question these monkeys. I belted one of the ginzos in the gut, flattened him. When the blonde opens her yap I told her to shut up. This crippled guy starts with, 'See here, you can't talk to ...'

"He moved one of his canes and I thought he was going to slug me and ... Oh, hell that's a crock—I was damn sore at him for laying this fine white stuff so I slapped him. When he fell he did swing at me with a cane and I kicked him in the side. The blonde came at me and I let her have it across the face—what she deserved. The ..."

"Marty Bond, cop, judge, brute, and little god!" Lawrence said suddenly, his voice so cold and sharp it made me jump.

"Somebody beat you to the punch tonight, called me a lout. And I only asked for money due me but ... All right, kid, I'm not saying aye nor nay at the moment, only telling you what the 'useful' years were like. This DeCosta babe screams at me, *You thug with a badge!*'

Told you, been dreaming about that, hearing the words lately, first time in years. To cut this short, the wops get scared and try making a run for it and for a second I'm belting everybody. We never had a chance to pin a thing on them, not even resisting arrest."

"Are you done?"

"No, I want to give you the complete picture, the full dose. Turns out the spick was an artist and a ship's radio officer who'd been hurt in a wreck. When I kicked him I knocked his spine out of whack. The blonde was a buyer for a department store, a big job. She sues the city for a hundred grand. Downtown had to back me up and we started giving her the works. First she lost her good job when the store found out she was married to a brown boy. It took over a year before the case reached court and we visited her every week, pleading, threatening. We got to her lawyer, threatened her landlord with violations, and he had them move. No papers would give them any publicity except the radical rags. The net result was the case never came up because she had a breakdown and was sent to an institution."

He opened his eyes, hard eyes. "What's the moral, Marty?" he asked bitterly. "When you see a robbery *don't* call the police?"

"I don't know what the moral is—I'm only telling you about one Marty Bond, the toughest cop out. The trouble with you, you think police work is like in the movies, clever, smart, and ..."

"You're the movie cop, taking a short cut, belting the 'truth' out of everybody! Marty Bond's version of old lady justice, a left to the gut!" His eyes were glaring at me, angry eyes.

"Maybe my version is the right one. You know me— the most decorated cop, the hero of small boys."

"Why don't you leave me alone?"

"I will. You see, Lawrence, I never thought of myself as a ... a ... bad guy, not even a nasty joker. But I suppose I was. After the DeCosta mess, Dot wouldn't have anything to do with me. Guess I wasn't her 'ideal' cop any longer. What she didn't understand is, I wasn't punch-happy—it's simply when you're going good you want to keep going at a fast clip. And most times I was right. Usually a person mixed up in a crime, no matter how, usually he's guilty. Take that Rogers-Graham case that got me bounced. I was ... "

He tried to turn his head away and couldn't; his eyes filled with pain. "I don't want to hear about it."

"I want you to hear about it. And I want to talk— makes me feel better. You see, boy, something happened to me a few days ago that set me to thinking about my life, my past."

"But I know all about that case—you made a mistake."

"I sure did. Only what you don't know is this: that Rogers bastard claimed I was out to get him. Well, that's the truth. You see he was one of these smart black boys. A young snot working as a delivery boy for a hardware store. Here's what you don't know about the case— about seven months before the mugging, I was called to Central Park West on a purse snatching. At ten in the morning some rich old biddy is on her way to the subway when she's knocked over by a guy in blue denim work pants—that's all she saw—and her purse is taken. She had ninety dollars in it. I got there a few minutes after it happened and there's Rogers, in blue dungarees, coming out of an apartment delivery entrance. I frisk him and he has a wad of seventy dollars on him—gave me some bull about a horse coming in for him. I cuffed him once and he stopped talking and I booked him. The biddy couldn't say if it was a white or colored guy who knocked her over, but she was sure of one lousy thing, the time—ten o'clock on the nose. So ..."

"Please, Marty, I don't ..."

"Shut up, and listen! You always liked to hear crime cases. This snotty Rogers don't deny anything but when he's arraigned in night court he calls the wife of a big magazine publisher who swears Rogers came up with a delivery and was repairing her baby carriage from nine-thirty till ten-fifteen. She's positive about the time because she had an appointment with the baby doctor at eleven and kept telling Rogers to hurry. The wise guy couldn't tell me that, made me look like a fool. The judge bawls me out, to make an impression on the publisher, and I told Rogers I'd get him. Months later when the guy was mugged and killed in the park, I went right over to the hardware store, found Rogers was out on a delivery near the park. I worked a confession out of him before we reached the station house, and even the one witness backed me up—all colored look alike. I got a tough break when they picked up Graham a year later and he started confessing to everything—including this killing. Papers played it up big and you know the rest—the department gave me a break, retired me fast. But I still think Rogers had something to do with the ..."

His eyes almost popped. "Marty, please, please—shut up!"

"I haven't even told you about some of my other cases, the ..."

He yelled, or maybe it was a sort of scream. A nurse came rushing in, along with the cop on duty. Lawrence said, "Get him out of here!"

The cop grabbed my arm and I jerked it away, walked out of the room. The cop followed me, asking, "What you trying to do?"

"What are you going to do about it?" Suddenly I felt

too tired to care. There was a funky taste in my mouth and I went over to the water fountain, then hit the sidewalk.

Along with a breath of cool air I got this sure feeling I was being tailed as I walked down Seventh Avenue. I stopped for a couple of hamburgers, some java, and a slice of watermelon. The taste of the onions on the hamburgers stayed with me as I rode back to the Grover.

As I came in, Kenny the bellhop called me over, said, "Been waiting for you, Marty. Some guy in shorts and a knapsack, one of them health nuts, registered this afternoon. Two more clowns in shorts went up to visit him, walked up—that was several hours ago."

Dewey came over. "They're in 419. Registered as a single."

"All right, I'll go up."

I knocked on 419 and didn't get any answer, so I used my pass key and almost stumbled over two jokers sleeping on the floor in sleeping bags.

They were all kids, under twenty, and the one on the bed, a crew-cut blond, said, "What is this? My friends are merely resting and ..."

"Cut it, chum. You got this room as a single for two and a half. Your friends want to rest, let them register, or pay another two and a half each."

The three kids were blushing and finally the one on the bed said, "Look, mister, we're hosteling, and we haven't much money. It's only one night. Can't you give us a break?"

"And if I lose my job because of this, who'll give me a break? Tell you what, pay another two and a half and you can stay here."

"Can we get a larger room?"

"Look, I can throw you all the hell out of here! A larger room is another five bucks. What's it going to be?"

The three clowns held a short conference, then got up two and a half. I told them, "Next time, don't try pulling any crap like this," and opened the door.

One of the crew-cuts sitting up in his sleeping bag asked, "Do we get a receipt?"

"You want one?" I asked, giving them the growl, stepping back into the room.

Blond-boy said quickly, "No, that's okay."

I went back down to the lobby, gave Kenny and Dewey a buck to split, went to my room and showered, even put powder between my toes—as though it made any diff if I got athlete's foot now.

Stretching out on the bed I listened to my belly rumble and thought about Lawrence, and if I'd been too rough on the kid. I'd only told him the truth, except for that line about rushing home to Dot. I was on my way to see a babe. But it still was the truth—I never two-timed Dot; nothing came of that night because I never got to see the babe.

The house phone buzzed. Dewey said, "Outside call for you, Marty." A second later Bill Ash asked, "Marty?"

"Aha. What's up?"

"Nothing much. Your former wife Flo called me, wanted your address. I gave her a line about I'd try and find it, to call me back in the morning. What shall I tell her?"

"Give her the Grover. Anything breaking on Lawrence?"

"No. We finally dug up a witness, some fishing bug named Bridgewater who lives across the street. He was practicing flycasting in his room and ..."

"He was what?"

"Told you he's a fishing nut. He was trying out a new reel, hitting the open window with the fly from across his room. He says he saw Lawrence—a cop—go into the hallway—and a couple seconds later, when he was casting again, he saw a tall man, well dressed, in a coconut straw, leaving the house. Didn't see his face, and of course didn't think anything about it at the time. It isn't much to go on."

"Smith is tall."

"For the love of tears, break it off, Marty! There's over two hundred thousand tall men in New York City."

"But if it had been a runt, that would rule Bob out. Now, we ..."

"Marty, Marty, slow down. I just came home, trying to take a bath, relax, so don't get me worked up. Ah ... Marty ... Flo ... uh ... what's this she said about you saying you expect to be dead by the end of the week?"

"What? Oh, that—I was jazzing around with her. You know, guys our age never know when the old ticker gives the final chug. Flo is the dramatic type."

"She sure is. Well, I'm going to get some rest now. You do the same. Yeah, don't get Lawrence excited. Don't know what you told him, but the hospital complained to us, and Dot is up in the air."

"You know how badge-happy he is. I was merely letting him in on some of the fine aspects of our trade. Take your bath, Bill."

We hung up and I lay on the bed, fanning myself with a newspaper. I glanced at the paper. Seems they still hadn't found Mr. Mudd, the mad bank robber. The rest of the paper was full of tripe about Cocky Anderson, so I went back to fanning myself, thought about Flo, about Bill taking the trouble to worry about me after we'd almost slugged each other. All the years we were a team Bill and I were good friends, yet never too close. He was married from the start, never chased around. And one cocktail was enough for Bill—said only an unhappy man drank. Might be something to that.

Closest I ever came to really making Bill's character was when we killed time by playing penny rummy. He'd make a stack of ten pennies, then pile the rest of his coppers into stacks even with the first one ... and then carefully count the pennies in each pile.

But Bill minded his own business, never said a word when I was tanked on the job, or when I made a fool of myself over a broad—that's enough to find in a friend. And the way he stuck to his plump Marge, a real pot. He never liked Dot and me busting up, and he sure couldn't figure Flo, although you could see his desire for her in his eyes. I remember once, when she hooked me into buying her a fur cape, Bill asked me, "What does she do right?"

"Bill, I look at her and there's *nothing* she can do wrong," I'd told him, but he couldn't understand that. He liked to think of himself as a "family man," but that was a lot of slop; to him a woman was part of the home, like a rug—once you got a rug you had a rug and that was it.

I reached over and picked up my wrist watch from the bed table. The band was almost rotten with sweat. It was after ten. I got up and started to get dressed, including my gun and a flash. I went out to the lobby and Dewey was totaling the day's phone charges. He said, "Still muggy. Sure wish it would rain and break this heat."

I took a linen-closet key from the key rack when he wasn't looking, told him, "I'm going to my room and I don't want to be disturbed."

"Starting that again, Marty?"

"I have some business to take care of, but if anybody asks I'm still in my room. I'll be back in about an hour or so."

"Marty, you know I'm not strong. What if somebody starts a rumpus?"

"Sock 'em with one of your wine bottles—a full one," I said, walking back toward the service elevator. There was a back entrance to the Grover that was rarely used— my tail might or might not be covering it, but at the moment I didn't want to see him.

I ran the elevator up to the eighth floor, quietly walked by an open door where Barbara and a girl named Jean were sipping iced tea and playing gin.

When the Grover was built, there had been an apartment house set smack up against one side of it. A fire is said to have wrecked this building back in 1910 and it was made over into business lofts. Two years ago we started missing a lot of linen till I found some jerky wino had noticed that the fire escape of the loft building at one point practically touched the window of the eighth-floor linen closet. I'd put a folding steel gate on the inside of the window.

The damn closet was full of hot stale air, and I was running sweat by the time I got the bars out of the way, the window open. It was a snap to step out on the dark fire escape, go over the roof, then down a rear fire escape. These industrial joints are deserted at night and this one was too small for a night watchman. Not a soul was on the street when I stepped out, my gun in my pocket.

I wiped the sweat from my hands and face, stopped at a drugstore to buy a package of mints and roll of tape, headed for Lande's store. They were unloading at the docks nearby and had the big lights on, but the rest of the street was deserted. I taped off a section of the door glass close to the lock, quietly busted this with my gun, put on my gloves, and stuck the pieces of glass and tape in my pocket. Then I reached through the hole and opened the door.

Inside I shut my eyes for a minute and when I opened them I could see pretty good in the semidarkness. I don't know what I expected to see or find, but I didn't see a damn thing—it looked like the inside of the Bay meat store. The icebox was a square room about 15' x 55' and I stepped inside and flashed the light a few times, covering all but a thin ray with my hand. There was a big grinding machine and a large flat tin pan for holding the chopped meat, scales, rows of empty shelves with long white enameled pans, meat hooks on the wall, a roll of liverwurst and one of salami hanging from two hooks. In one corner there was a pile of canned hams, and under the chopped meat table I saw a box of smoked tongues. There was a light layer of fresh sawdust covering the floor. And a clean chopping block with knives and a cleaver stuck in one end of the block.

Everything looked all right—the trouble was I didn't know enough about the butcher business to know what "all wrong" would be.

But at least it was comfortably cool inside the icebox and through a window I could watch the store and the street. The hams came from Germany and being so close to the docks, Lande could be running a dope depot. I took a cleaver and busted open one of the cans of ham, split a smoked tongue in half. The tongue tasted fine. The ham was all cold grease—but ham.

I took the busted ham and tongue out with me and it was like stepping into a damp oven. I opened the door of the freezer next to the icebox. No light came on, but a cold blast of air gave me the creeps. Fumbling along the wall I found a switch, and the light went on. I jumped inside and slammed the door shut—through the open door of the freezer the light could be seen from the street.

There wasn't any window in the freezer and I didn't like the deal—if anybody had been following me, or if the broken door glass should be discovered, I was up the creek—a cold one. Anyway, I wasn't sweating about it—it was too damn cold. My breath turned to fog and my head felt like an icicle.

The freezer was loaded with meats—steaks, cans of livers, pork loins, tripe, pig's feet, turkeys and chickens—all of them frozen stiff and neatly packed in plastic bags with tags on them. From the wall hooks large turkeys and sides of meat hung, all wrapped in bags. On the sawdust floor I saw large wooden and cardboard boxes full of slabs of fat, pig's knuckles, cans of lard. I tried opening one of the bags of steak, but the meat was hard as a rock.

It was so cold I could barely breathe and every time I glanced at the thick door I felt like I was locked in a tomb. I unscrewed the bulb and there was a bad moment when I finally found the door and couldn't open it. You had to press the handle hard and hit the door with your shoulder. I came tumbling out into the dark store, shook for a second with a chill, then the muggy heat got me and I started to sweat, or thaw out.

I shut the door and the boom of the door closing filled the store and I stood very still for a moment, hand on my gun. But everything was all right. I went into Lande's office, pulled out two drawers and took them back into the freezer, screwed the light on. All I saw was bills and orders. I went through his checkbook and everything looked okay. These wholesale cats even had a daily news bulletin giving them the names of all restaurants and stores being sued.

I screwed the light off, went out and put the drawers back, picked up some mail and a cashbox, went back to my ice den. There was a key sticking in the tin cashbox and about six bucks in change, petty-cash vouchers for stamps and string. The mail seemed all ads and bills. I went out, slamming the door in a hurry so the light wouldn't be seen, returned the box and mail to the office. The store was a bust as far as I was concerned, although if he was running dope that would be the link, and you can have a fortune of the junk in a pound candy box.

I took the ham and the tongue, made sure the street was empty, then stepped out and walked up Front Street. I dumped the glass and tape from the door down a sewer opening, left the tongue and the open can of ham atop a garbage can—if the cats didn't get it, the market bums would when they made rounds, collecting for their Mulligan stew.

Via the fire escapes I got back into the Grover, put the gloves, flash, and gun in my room, then walked casually out to the desk. I'd been gone exactly an hour and thirty-three minutes. "How's things?" I asked Dewey.

"Nothing much. Marty, this Doc Dupre called again. Why don't you call him and get him off my back? You owe him money?"

"He wants his pound of flesh, rotten flesh," I said, enjoying my own little joke again and suddenly realizing that for the first time in days, at the moment I felt swell, no stink in my mouth, no tight feeling in my gut.

Dewey said, "Also, I keep telling you to call King. He said to call him at his house tonight."

"All right, you told me. Dewey, anybody check in today?" If my tail was a clever slob he, might be stopping at the Grover.

"Those kids. And a trucker."

"The trucker—old customer?"

"Yeah, the fat one who hustles watermelons up from Georgia."

"Where's your empty-room check sheet?"

He arched the shaggy eyebrows over his watery eyes. "One minute you're stroking the duck, the next you're an eager beaver. Here's the sheet."

"Dewey, I want a favor. Keep your bottle under the desk, don't go into the back room tonight, don't leave the desk. If anybody looks funny, or if anybody registers, call me in my room at once."

"In a jam?"

"I don't know, could be."

I went into the office and phoned King at his house. He shrilled, "It's near eleven—what do you mean by calling me so late, Bond?"

"Want me to hang up?"

"See here, Bond, I'm sick of your high-handed ways. Either you stay on the job or ..."

"Oh what? King, people in glass cat houses shouldn't talk so loud, or make any trouble."

"How dare you talk to me like that? I'll have you thrown out of your room and ...!"

"I didn't call to hear you blow your nose. Listen, King, far as you're concerned I'm on vacation for a few days, so stop pestering me, keep out of my way."

"As manager of the Grover, neither I nor the office will stand for such impertinence from ...!"

"Bag of bones, I won't tell you twice to stop running your mouth. As for that fancy office, tell them I'm coming down and underneath all the gold lettering on the door, where it says real estate, appraisals, insurance, I'll add ... pimping. Now, don't make waves!" I hung up, then went from floor to floor, starting with the check room in the basement, full of a lot of old trunks and boxes, checking the empty rooms. It isn't hard to sneak into a hotel, especially the fourth-rate ones, and there's little chance of getting caught if you only stay a night.

The rooms were okay. I dropped into the girls' room. Barbara was playing cards with a new babe—a tall strong blonde who looked fresh from the farm. Barbara asked, "Marty, where you been? Still feeling punk?"

"I'm okay. Who's this?"

"Agnes. A friend of Harold's is breaking her in and since Florence was sick tonight, Harold sent her."

"Isn't Jean here?"

"Sure, she's working. Why?"

I went over to the closet. Next to Barbara's square makeup bag—"like all the show girls have"—there was a small cardboard suitcase that would be Agnes's. As I opened it the big blonde asked, "What's the idea? Who you?"

"'Who you?' is Marty the house dick," Barbara told her. "What you looking for, Marty?"

There wasn't much in the bag—a dress, stockings, a change of underwear. If this was the syndicate I was wrestling with, a woman hood wasn't impossible.

Agnes came over and asked again, "What's the idea, lumpy?"

"Watch your mouth, honey," I told her, "or you'll be packing your vaseline and on your way out of here." I put the suitcase back and walked out into the hall—only had to wait a moment before Barbara came out, asked, "What's wrong, Marty?"

"Nothing, thought she might be a junkie. You know this hick?"

"I've seen her before, if that's what you mean."

I squeezed her hand. "All right, that's good enough for me."

"Ain't like you to be jumpy. Something up? Hope there ain't going to be a damn raid. I hate the ..."

"Everything is okay, honey." Looking at her closely I saw the remains of a black eye expertly covered by make-up. "Rough customer?" I pointed at the eye.

"Harold. He never understands that when it's so hot and muggy, business slumps. I'm glad you're back. I feel better with you around."

"I bet you tell that to all the boys."

She gave me a startled look, burst out laughing. "Get you, old two-ton turning coy." She dug a finger into my stomach. "Seriously, you know what I mean."

"All right," I said, to say something.

She dug a finger again. "You're losing weight, Marty." She slapped my pockets. "Knew you'd forget it."

"Forget what?"

"The perfume you promised me."

"You're wrong, I did buy it, but it broke in my pocket." I took out a couple of bucks. "Do me a favor and buy it yourself. You know what you want."

She shook her head. "It won't mean nothing unless you buy it, even if it comes from the dime store. Let me get back to Agnes—she's jittery. Hey, who's the scouts we got here with short pants?"

"Couple of health nuts. They ain't got a buck between them, so leave them alone. Don't work too hard, honey." I put the keys back on the office rack, went to my room. I set the alarm for seven in the morning, took another shower, and went to bed. I felt good, like my old self. I wondered if I was being overcautious, but then I didn't want my boy Smith to find out I didn't know a thing, and lay off me. Although Lande would be bait any time I wanted Bob to come running—if it was Bob. Only it had to be him, and he'd do *that* little favor for me. I wanted a cigarette and a shot, decided to hell with it, dropped off into a deep sleep.

About a half hour later the phone buzzed and I had to jerk myself up a thousand yards of good sleep before I managed to sit up, growl, "What the hell you want?"

Dewey said, "A guy just registered."

"So what?"

"You off your noggin, Marty? Didn't you tell me to let you know if anybody registered?"

"All right, all right, this a new customer?"

"Never saw him before. Well dressed."

"Where is he?"

"Room 431. Name is Al Berger. In from Stamford City. No baggage and paid in advance, of course."

I dressed, wore my gun, and went up and knocked on 431. A young guy, lean build, opened the door—the type that could be anything. He had his coat and tie off, and his white shirt was damp with sweat. There was a shadow of a line running across his chest—the kind of indentation the strap from a shoulder holster could make. He looked me over coolly, asked, "What do you want?"

"I'm the house dick—want to be sure everything is okay," I said, pushing the door open, spinning him around and bending his arm up behind his back before he knew what the play was.

He sort of yelled, "What the hell is this?" He was so damn scared I knew I'd made a wrong move. But I had to bluff it out or he could sue the Grover, although I didn't know why I should care, so I snapped, "Got a license to carry a gun?"

"What gun?"

"That's a holster crease across your shirt."

"A what? I ... oh, for ... that's from the strap of my gadget case. It's on the bed."

I glanced over at the bed and there was one of those leather bags camera nuts sport their gear in. I gave him a quick frisk, let him go. He rubbed his arm for a second, then pulled out his wallet, showed me a card in some photographers' society, then an announcement that the society was meeting in New York City.

"Sorry, Mr. Berger, I made a mistake. But we run a respectable hotel and I have to ..."

"I know how respectable—a girl solicited me in the hallway a few minutes ago!"

"I'll correct that. You see, you look like a guy that caused trouble here once before. No harm done. I apologize, Mr. Berger," I said, crawfishing out of the room.

Kenny took me down to the main floor. I wondered what in hell I was so jumpy about—even if it was Bob, he would only be mildly curious about me. But if he was tailing me ...

The door to my room was ajar and I couldn't remember if I'd left it closed or not. I sure was losing my touch. I stood there for a moment wondering if I should take my gun out—I was only in this to stop a slug. But I'd talked myself into getting Bob Smith at the same time, if I could.

I took the gun out of the holster, put it in my pocket as I inched the door open. Harold was sitting on my bed, smoking a pipe and reading the morning paper. I asked, "What you doing in my room?"

He didn't look up, merely nodded as he muttered, "Your door was open, Marty. I knew you wouldn't be in the sack so early. Not yet midnight."

I closed the door. He kept on reading the paper. Harold didn't look like a pimp, although few look like the movie version; the greasy joker with an evil handsome face. I always figured all pimps as part queer.

Harold didn't even go for sharp clothes. He was a fat, thick-necked guy who looked like a longshoreman. He was wearing a crumpled white sport shirt and cheap slacks, blue canvas shoes. The only thing queer about him was his long dark hair which he kept wet and carefully brushed, every hair in place. Of course Harold was also queer for expensive cars.

I walked over to the bed and he folded the paper, started in with, "Marty, we got us a sweet little racket here, quiet and hidden away. Everybody is taken care of—be silly for any of us to spoil it or ..."

"Barbara call you?"

"That Barbara acting up? Giving you any trouble? King called me. He was upset."

"Tell him to lay off me. Also tell your mudkickers to stop soliciting in the hallways. Kenny and Dewey get them enough business. And quit socking Barbara—black eyes don't look good in the romance racket. Now, get out, I'm sleepy."

"No rush, Marty old man, we haven't talked for a ..."

"Where do you get off, old-manning me?" I said, hooking him in the belly with my right. I may have lost my touch, but my punch was still there—Harold shot off the other side of the bed, landed on his head, and did a clumsy somersault before he spread out on the carpet. His fat mouth was fish-spread, fighting for air. I was waiting for him to sit up so I could clip him again—for Barbara—but I decided that would only make the jerk beat her more. I had a better idea.

Taking the scissors from the bathroom, I cut off as much of his hair as I could, a chunk here, a chunk there, while he moaned, "No ...! Aw, Marty.... No!" I didn't know which was hurting him more, his belly or the sight of the hair on the floor.

"Harold, it's easier on your puss and my hands than if I belted you around. Now, stay the hell out of my room, out of my way." I dragged him up by one shoulder, dumped him in the hallway, locked the door. Making sure the alarm was set, I undressed and dropped off into a fine sleep.

I didn't need any alarm to get me up at seven—I was

up before that, coughing and sneezing, running a temperature, with the worst damn summer cold I ever had.

My head was stuffed, and my eyes and nose running. Between sneezes, as I dressed, I got down a fine hooker of rye and almost laughed—my gut felt fine and my mouth was sweet—so I was probably dying of pneumonia!

It was dawn outside and Sam wasn't open yet. The streets were almost deserted, only a few cars parked, and I slowly walked my sniffles over to Hamilton Square. I bought some paper handkerchiefs and a box of cough drops in a cigar store, certain I wasn't being followed. I had some java, eggs and bacon, then took a cab over to the middle of Twelfth Street. I got out and walked slowly toward Fifth Avenue. The street was asleep. No car nor man followed me. I got another cabbie, had him take me up to Twenty-third Street, then downtown. I took a plant behind some parked trailers, watching Lande's place, eating the box of cough drops and wiping my nose every few minutes.

I was still there at nine—not sure Lande would show. I bought some oranges from a guy with a pushcart and felt better. My fever seemed gone and except for my running nose, I felt pretty good.

At a quarter to ten an old station wagon parked in front of the meat store and Lande got out. He was halfway across the sidewalk when he saw the hole in his door. He ran into the store.

Exactly eleven minutes later he rushed out and looked up and down the street—for a cop—then dashed back into the store. A few minutes later a radio car came screaming to a stop and two cops jumped out.

I walked away, stopped for a hot dog and bottle of soda, then went up to Sam's. I felt a little foolish. I'd been certain Lande wouldn't call the cops.

I wondered what I'd done with the cereal—for I felt I was acting like a junior G-man with a box-top badge.

Five

Sam gave me penicillin tablets and a slug of medicine that tasted like stale Scotch. "That will knock it out, Marty. If it doesn't, see a doctor. You got yourself a real cold. I … uh … trust you've been careful with those sleeping pills."

"Threw them away. You're right, Sam, why mess with that stuff."

The relief almost oozed over Sam's heavy face. "That was smart. Go back to the hotel and get some sleep. Best thing for a cold. You look awful sad."

"I don't feel exactly overbright," I said.

He started gabbing about a fight he'd watched on TV the night before. I didn't listen, for in the back of my head I had this feeling something was out of place.

"…There's this big muscle-bound dope with his knees buckling. Instead of staying away, what does he but come in. Wham! He's clipped again by the right and it's all over. I'm telling you, Marty, pugs today don't know their business."

"Yeah, it's always easier to know what to do when you're outside the ring," I told him. "I remember …" All of a sudden I felt good—Lande had played it the way I figured, after all! The damn cold must have had me groggy—it was eleven minutes before he came out of the shop, looked for a cop. Then he went back in and phoned the police. That meant he'd called somebody else first, had been told to call the cops.

It fitted—I was still in business—even if I didn't know what business.

"As you were saying ...?"

"Nothing, except sometimes it's tough to think in the clinches. I'll see you, Sam."

I was in business but still in the dark about the link between the syndicate and a small-timer like Lande. I went back to see the driver again. He was packing a truck, told me to wait a few minutes. He was wearing what looked like a motorcycle racer's lined leather hat, only it was too big for him and he looked like the comic in an old burlesque.

He was busy taking slabs of fat out of the freezer and when he finished he said, "I got about ten minutes for talk," and pulled off the hat, ran a comb through his thick hair. He looked at the comb, said, "Lousy hat is dirty."

"Hot for a hat," I said, wiping my nose.

He laughed. "I feel for you. Nothing as uncomfortable as a summer cold. And the freezer is the place to get one. Stay in there for a few minutes without a hat and you'll get yourself a hell of a cold. Some of the brain juices freeze."

"Stop it. You mean you shake your noggin and hear the icicles rattle?"

"I sure do mean it," this Lou said. "Guys that work in the freezer keep every part of them covered, including a muffler over their faces. Let me take you in, show you how cold it is."

"I believe you. What they need a freezer for? Special meats that won't keep in the icebox?" I asked, and I had a fair idea what the link was—the punks must have been reading too many detective yarns. This was an old gimmick, although I'd never heard of it being actually used except in the movies and books.

"Look, you buy a case of turkeys or a side of beef, whatever it is, it don't move. After a few days in the icebox the meat starts getting 'slick'—a little slimy. It's about a day from turning. You toss it in the freezer, keep it till you get a call for turkeys."

"Freezing make them any better?"

"No better, no worse. Soon as they thaw out they're as good as they were when you put them in. We keep them covered in bags so the skin won't get a freezer burn. Before they had freezers, the butchers were forced to buy carefully or throw out ..."

"All right, Lou," I cut in, "I'll never be in the meat business. Tell me, has Willie been around to see you since we last talked?"

Franconi shook his head. "Should he have?"

"Yes and no. I'll level with you, Lou. I been fishing and not coming up with anything. Looks like my hunch has worn thin."

"Like I told you, Willie hasn't the iron to be crooked. How's the cop that was slugged?"

"He'll live. Do any ship stewards buy supplies from Lande? He's right on the water front."

Lou grinned. "Mister, you ain't even warm. Supplying ships is real big business. Willie would give both arms to be able to get in that."

"Lande have any sailor friends? Maybe from the old country, dropping in to visit him?"

"Willie had no time for any friends. What's all this salt air about?"

"Like I said, fishing. I thought Willie might be mixed up in a dope deal."

"Pal, you're way off base."

"How do you know—for sure? He could have a hundred grand worth of heroin in a box smaller than a canned ham."

"It ain't like that, mister. Aside from Willie not going in for phony deals, I'm with him all morning, part of

the afternoon. And every other night I sweep and mop
down the joint—ain't a spot in the shop I ain't cleaned.
I even help him with the books. He couldn't hide any-
thing from me. I'm like a partner, except for the dough.
If I ever hit a horse or a number I'm going to suggest to
Willie we become real partners."

"Suggest it to his wife—Willie may not be around too
long. What about the wife—any boy friends?"

"You ain't ever seen Bebe, or you wouldn't ask that.
All spread and a yard wide. Lucky she has Willie."

"Well, thanks, Lou. Remember, keep your mouth shut
about our little talks."

"They couldn't beat a word out of me."

"Don't be too sure of that. That's why I want you not
to tell anybody about our talks. Maybe I'll see you
again."

"My wife gives the kid a lot of brown sugar in warm
milk for a cold—try it. How did you get yours?"

"It was so hot last night I stuck my head in the ice-
cube tray," I cornballed, walking up the street. I hadn't
gone a hundred yards when I got that old feeling I was
being followed, like a hound dog striking a scent. This
street was a cinch for a shadow. It was full of cars and
trucks and people.

I dropped into a candy store, phoned Bill Ash. After
we said it was a hell of a hot day and I found out how
Lawrence was—he was up and around in a wheel
chair—Bill said, "Got something in your mouth—voice
sounds funny."

"All I got in my mouth is a lousy cold. Bill, will you
humor an ancient cop and put a tail on a Lou Franconi?
He's Lande's driver and working now at the Bay Meat
Company, a wholesale outfit. And do it fast."

"Is it okay if I ask why?"

"I'm sure somebody is tailing me, and like a clown I

just led the tail to Franconi. We did a lot of talking out on the sidewalk. He's a nice kid and I don't want to see him slugged. Only need a man on him for a day or two."

"Still playing cop, Marty?"

"Aha, and the game's getting interesting."

"I got something that should interest you. Your buddy Lande's shop was broken into last night. You playing burglar too?"

"Why should I bust into his store? Too hot to eat meat. Anyway, he was only taken for a canned ham and a tongue. Bill, you going to put a man on the kid—right now?"

"Okay, but it seems like a wild goose ... How did you know only a ham and a tongue was lifted? Marty, I want to see you damn quick! You're not here in ten minutes I'll bring you in!"

"You're slow this morning, Sherlock Holmes. I was waiting for you to make that sharp deduction. Frankly, I was surprised Lande went to the cops—almost upset all of my bright deductions. Don't forget a man on Franconi, and make it fast because he's starting on a delivery route."

"I want to see you right away!"

"On my way up. I'm serious, Bill. Put a man on the kid."

"For the love of tears, I said I would. Now drag your rusty up here on the double."

"At the moment my rusty is higher off the ground than yours. I'll be up in a few minutes."

I walked slowly to the station house, considering going out to Jones Beach for a dip and some surf casting. Except for fishing I was never an outdoor man, but with only a day or two left, there were a lot of "last" things I ought to do. Still it was a relief to know I'd never *have* to do a damn thing again.

Bill looked worse than poorly; all the dapperness had fallen away. As I sat down he began, "Marty, I warned you to stop acting like a goddam tin hero. Breaking into …"

"Stop it, Bill. No one knows about it."

"I know about it!"

"Then forget it. What did Lande lose—a busted door glass, a couple of pounds of meat. He's probably insured. Relax, Bill, you look tired,"

Bill rubbed his chin. "I've never been so tired—can't go for two or three days steady any longer. Thought I'd get some rest last night, but the girl was sick with her virus and you know how up in the air Margie gets when there's sickness. Tell me, Humphrey Bogart, what did you find in that store besides meat?"

"Nothing but a cold."

"I don't understand you. In the old days you never broke your back over anything—here you work like a pig over nothing. Still think you're being tailed?"

"I know I am. Bill, I know I'm acting nuts, but there's too many coincidences in this for me to be drawing a complete blank. The kid being beaten after sticking his nose into Lande's business—that now-you-see-it, now-you-don't fifty grand—and now me being tailed."

"What does the guy look like?"

"I've never been able to spot him—just have this feeling."

Bill jumped up, started walking the room. "Jeez, you have a *feeling?* Marty, I just wasted a man on this Franconi when I doubly need every man I have. And your Mr. Lande, he's ready for a padded cell—never saw a guy so nervous."

"Why do you think he's so jumpy?"

Bill gave me a long look. "You're acting like a damn

school kid! He finds his store's been entered. Why shouldn't he be nervous? Marty, for old times' sake, or for any reason you want, wait till I get off this Cocky Anderson hook. Then you can play cops and robbers all you wish. The case is driving me batty without any help from you."

"See by the papers you're no place."

"Lousy papers. I've tried everything and can't get a lead worth peanuts. I've never been a third-degree loon, but I'd like to give Bochio a taste of the rubber hose! He's too sure of himself. Even with his alibi he should be more careful than these statements about he's sore somebody beat him to the punch, and all the rest of the slop that makes good headline reading."

"Bochio still down in Florida?"

Ash nodded, rubbed his neck. "What can we bring him back on? That's another crazy angle. You always stumble upon some strong lead, even if it proves a dead end later. But in this case we don't come across a damn thing. And I've squeezed and pushed everybody who might know a damn thing. So has Homicide. Nobody knows a thing!"

"I'd still bring Bochio up—try talking to him."

"Talk to him about what, shooting off his mouth? He knows we don't have a thing. Bring him up and we'll have to turn him loose in a minute, make us look like fools. The smart louse has even *volunteered* to come back to New York if we ask him to!"

"These wogs are oily jokers."

Bill stopped pacing the office, stood in front of me shaking his head sadly. "Marty, sometimes I wonder how you were ever lucky enough to break the cases you did, with a mind as narrow as a pipe cleaner. For what it's worth, Bochio *isn't* Italian."

"With a handle like that? I always thought he was."

"His real name is Boch—and don't tell me all Dutch-men are oily jokers. He was raised by an Italian family from the time he was a kid. That's where he got the accent from, and they added an 'io' to his name and he had it legally changed to Bochio a long time ago. He's married to an Italian girl, considers himself Italian, and ..."

I sneezed, a hell of a sneeze that shook my toes, near tore Bill's little office apart. He jumped back, ran a hand over his face. "You pig. Told you my girl was sick. Why don't you cover your mouth?"

I was on my way to the door. "Be grateful for that sneeze. It rattled my brains—could be the break in the Anderson case."

Bill's long face seemed to sag as he touched my arm, said, "Marty, why don't you see a doctor?"

"I already have. Be good and maybe I'll give you Cocky Anderson's killer all bound up in pink handcuffs," I said, walking out.

In the old days when a case broke it was like being on a drinking jag, the same high feeling. Now it didn't do a thing to me except amaze me how a little thing always trips a big deal.

I didn't have proof yet, but the way the pieces were falling into place, I knew it had to be the link. The secret of police work is digging into every fact—and Bill had overlooked a couple of small ones, just as I had. And of course, you got to have luck—like my chewing the fat with Bill and him breaking things right over my head, without knowing it.

It took me a couple of dimes and a quart of sweat in a phone booth to get ahold of the guy at Immigration again. He said he'd check and call me back at the Grover after lunch.

I had time to kill and because it was on my list of "last

things," I took a cab to the Battery and the ferry to Staten Island, the cheapest and most interesting voyage in the country.

In Staten Island I went into a spaghetti joint and had a pizza pie and a couple of glasses of beer. There were a dozen or so guys eating in the joint and I wondered if my tail was among them. But it didn't matter; I had him on a string and he'd jump whenever I yanked it.

I was back in the Grover by one and Lawson told me, "I wish you would stay around to take care of your personal business, Bond. A Dr. Dupre has been calling you every hour. And a rather striking-looking woman was here, left this number for you to call. She claimed she was your ex-wife."

I crumbled the paper with Flo's number. "What do you mean, claimed?"

"How a gorgeous woman would ever fall for you is beyond my ken."

"Your what? Look, nancy, don't let it worry you—you'll never get within fondling distance of anything like Flo, and if you did, you wouldn't know what to do. I'm expecting a call—put it right through to my room."

"Mr. King is in the office."

"Who cares!"

I was feeling so good I overdid it—in my room I knocked off a big slug of rye for no reason and my belly began acting up, as if to remind me of the reason I was in the deal.

Shortly before two Barbara dropped into my room and when I asked why she was at work so early, she said, "I never went home last night. Gee, Marty, you shouldn't have cut Harold's hair. He thinks you're sore at me and if I'd gone home last night he would have whipped the hide off me."

"Going home tonight?"

"Maybe," she said, pouring herself a small one.

"Look, you take one of the rooms here—perma-
nently—and if that fat punk tries to ..." I stopped talking.
I wouldn't be around much longer to take care of
Harold, or anybody else. It was an odd feeling, like
somebody had pulled me up short.

Barbara finished the drink. "Thanks for worrying, but
it will be okay when I go home tonight with two days'
dough. With Harold, I always got to build him up—he
has to be the big I-am. And money is the best builderup-
per. I did swell last night—a ten-buck tip. Nice-dressed
guy—asked about you."

"About ...? What did he ask?"

"Nothing exactly, but a whole lot. I pegged him for a
racket-fellow. I think he was casing the setup here, but
then he got off on you—how long had you been here,
you have any side jobs, any dough? Lot of questions
that didn't add up. He knew about you being on the
force. You know me, I knew from nothing."

"What did he look like?"

"Big, hard body, out-of-towner with a twang. Sort of
good looking in a ..."

"Look like Dick Tracy?"

She stretched all her lipstick in a large grin. "Say, I
kept thinking he reminded me of somebody and that's
it—Dick Tracy, all them sharp features, hat low on his
head."

"What time was all this?"

"Oh ... about one, two. Why you so interested?"

"Why didn't you call me, or tell me?"

"Marty, you toss Harold out and he tells me to stay
away from you. And you been so grouchy these days
and I figured you were asleep. Anyway, the guy wasn't
tough or nothing, very friendly and casual like."

"He use the word *bastid*? Not *bas-tard* but ...?"

Barbara stiffened. "Please, what kind of conversation you think we were having?"

She wasn't kidding, so I let it drop. "Dewey see him come in?"

"How do I know? But that wino was off last night, stinking, and I know Kenny had to run the elevator and cover for him most of the night. Gee, Marty, so a guy asked about you—all friendly-like. What's so important about all this?"

"Nothing." That had been a slip on my part, not alerting Kenny. Dewey, the damn lush! And last night, Smith probably didn't know about the store being broken into, so he was just looking around. Must be puzzled as hell about me sticking my nose in things.

"Marty, you angry with me?" Barbara asked, playing coy, coming over and putting her hand on my shirt, making it stick to my damp skin.

"No, honey. Wait here for a couple of minutes. I'll be back."

"Mind if I take a shower? I smell like a couple of other gals."

"Take a brace of showers," I said, going out. I called Sam from the desk, asked what his most expensive perfume cost. It was twenty-seven bucks with taxes and I told him to send over a bottle right away.

Lawson was on the elevator with King keeping an eye on the desk. He came out of the office, told me, "Mr. Bond, it's time we had a little talk. You have not only been impertinent, but also negligent in your duties as a ..."

I went over to him. His skin was waxy and drawn tight over his bony puss. "Why don't you change your record? You're an old man and I guess you want to live longer, although I can't figure why or ..."

"You can't bully me!" He actually made his little hands

into fists.

"Yes, I can, King. I can bully you all I want because if I feel like it, I'll belt that funny-looking chin of yours, bust all the bones, including your store choppers. I can do that with one punch, one good ..."

"Roughneck!" He almost screamed the word at me as he retreated into his office.

I don't know what it was, maybe the hatred in his eyes, but it was like looking into a crystal ball, seeing my life, and that one word, "roughneck," summed it up. Roughneck, lout, bully ... they covered the years, my lousy stupid life, all of it. It made me feel crummy.

King got courage, and some color back in his face, stuck his stickpin head out of the office door. "You think you can push me around because you're all muscles. Well, there will be an accounting soon that will ...!"

"All right, don't crowd your luck with a roughneck," I growled, and walked to the front of the small lobby, sat down, wondering why the cockroach had upset me— and he had. I sat there for maybe ten minutes, thinking of nothing, almost wanting to bawl.

Sam came over himself and I paid him for a bottle that looked like a watch charm, it was that small, but Sam wasn't the kind to gyp me. He asked if my cold was better, told me to drop over for some more pills.

Back in my room I found Barbara dressing. I placed the tiny box in her hands as she pulled on her dress, asked, "What's this?"

"A time bomb—what does it look like?"

She unwrapped it and stared at the little bottle, then up at me, and began to cry a little. "Lord, Marty, this is Arpège!"

"Sure is," I said, as if I knew what she was talking about.

"I've bought the toilet water but ... this is the perfume!"

She came over and gave me a sloppy kiss, whispered, "Hon, it's been a long time for us."

"Sure, but you just took a shower, no sense getting sweated up. Some other time."

She pulled away, rubbed her nose with the bottle. "You're a funny one—lately. Before you were so tough and ..."

"Being tough is a lot of crap," I said, slapping her hips.

"... and now you're sentimental."

"You bet I am. We've had some good times together. And being sentimental over a whore is getting down to the tacks of life."

"Why did you have to use that word, Marty?"

"Why not? We never kidded ourselves. Let old poppa Marty tell you what I've learned the last few days—this is a whoring world and it makes us all whores in one way or another."

Barbara slipped me the coy look again. "I suppose what you said is awful deep or something; I'll have to think about it. Marty, was the girl asking for you this morning really your wife?"

"Yeah."

"She looks like what I used to dream about when I was a kid—being real big-time, real beautiful."

"You should have seen her eight or nine years ago."

"No, she looks beautiful now because she knows she isn't any kid and still she has it—what a figure."

"Maybe she was too pretty."

"How come you let something like that go?"

I slapped Barbara's hips again. "Something like that let me go. But by then it didn't matter. Flo was like a pug in training—all the time. Couldn't do this or that because it might spoil her figure, surf casting roughened her skin ... all that. Now she wants me back and she has a swell setup."

"No wonder you've been fluffing the duff here—you're going back to her."

"No, it's too late for that." I was suddenly bored with all the small talk. "Honey, want to take a walk, or something? I need some shut-eye."

"Okay. Thanks for the perfume. Guess it is too muggy to do anything but sleep."

When she left I sat on the bed, wondering how to kill the afternoon—my last afternoon. Be good to get drunk, but with my gut it might spoil things for tonight—and it was going to be tonight. Jones Beach was too much effort and ...

The phone rang—my boy in Immigration. He told me what I expected, and of course it fitted, as I knew it would. There it was, all wrapped up. I could pull the string now by merely calling Bill—they'd make him a captain at least for this—only there was my own very special angle, the only thing that mattered for me.

I still had the rest of the afternoon and my room depressed me. I went out and Lawson asked, "Where you going, Bond?"

"I'm going to break your nosy head!" I said, making for the desk.

He backed into the office. "I'm only asking in case you get any calls."

"Tell them I'm out counting the pansies in Washington Square," I said, turning toward the door.

I walked over to Seventh Avenue, stopped for pie and iced coffee. I was still being tailed. I decided to tell Lawrence good-by.

The doc wasn't happy to see me, said, "Mr. Bond, you upset him badly the last time you were here. I'll find out if he wants to see you."

He returned in a few minutes to tell me I could go in. "But please make it brief and be careful what you say— no arguments."

The same cop was on the door and he gave me a hard look as I went in. The boy was in a wheel chair, tape over his nose, the top of his head bandaged. He was bare to his waist although most of his ribs were taped. I said, "Well, kid, you're coming along fine."

"That's what they tell me." His eyes seemed to be studying me. "Glad you came by, Marty. I've thought over what you told me—I'm still going to become a cop—at least try to. I'll be a good cop if for no other reason because I'll stop any other Marty Bonds from abusing their authority."

I shrugged. "You do that, Lawrence—if you can. All right, if you're still badge-happy, pass the exam and they'll welcome you with open arms."

"Is this another of your ... uh ... jokes?"

"Kid, you stumbled on the hottest thing going. You stick to your story; you *always* knew this was big."

"I don't understand you."

"You will by morning. And don't be modest. Blow your horn loud. The cops wouldn't listen, but you knew there was something fishy about Lande from the go. Don't rap the department, but don't let the reporters forget you. I'm giving you full credit for ..."

"You've cracked it?"

"By tomorrow you and I will have cracked New York City wide open. Now don't ask no more questions— just wait." I shook his hand. "So long, kid."

"Marty, what's all this about?"

"You'll know tomorrow. I hope this beating has taught you something, but I doubt it. Maybe it may teach you not to learn things the hard way. Good-by, Lawrence." I let go of his hand.

"But, Marty ...? Wait!"

I opened the door as he called, "Dad—wait!" I closed the door softly, winked at the cop, and walked out onto Seventh Avenue.

It was a few minutes after three and for no reason I walked across the street and bought a ticket for Loew's Sheridan, lost myself in the darkness. It was cool and the movie was one of these color jobs shot over in Europe, and I got a kick out of seeing the streets of Rome and Naples I remembered from the war. The story was silly as hell and the other feature had Hollywood winning the West from the Indians for the millionth time. I chewed mints and worked on my running nose, wondered if my shadow was enjoying the pictures.

It was almost seven when I came out into the hot end of the day, feeling rather sorry for myself—a guy who didn't know what to do with his last hours but spend them seeing slop on the screen.

I walked over to Eighth Street and had a good seafood supper. It was a big meal and didn't seem to bother my gut, although when I reached the Grover I had to dash for the john. I came back to the lobby, shut off the radio in the office. Dewey came in from the desk. "Hey, I'm listening to a story."

"Take the radio out to the desk, I have some typing to do. I told you to lay off the back room last night—a guy came in while you were getting your wine chilled."

"That's a lot of nonsense. I never left ... How did you know?"

"Forget it and get out of here."

It took me an hour to peck out a letter, with a carbon, telling Bill how Bochio had knocked off Cocky Anderson. I played up Lawrence big in my report. I even suggested sweating Willie for the exact details. After I sealed it, I wrote my name over the back of the envelope so

Dewey's curiosity wouldn't get the best of him, put Bill's name on the front, along with the phone number of the station house.

I went to my room and shaved and showered like a bridegroom. Dropping some weight made me look in shape—on the outside I looked healthier than I had since I was a teenage punk. I made sure my gun was in working order before I slipped it and some extra shells into my pocket. I dragged an old suitcase from the closet, took out my army .45 which I'd smuggled into civilian life, checked it, strapped it above my right ankle.

It was eight-twenty and starting to get dark. One thing worried me—Laude might not be home when I phoned him. He could easily be at a movie, or something. But he'd have to come home sooner or later.

Out in the lobby I motioned for Kenny to take over the desk and walked Dewey to my room. He took a swig of the pint of sherry in his hip pocket as he sat down, asked, "Now, what's cooking?"

"We're cooking without wine. Dewey, when you finish that pint, that's going to be all for the night."

"You a reformer now, too?"

I pulled out all the bills I had in my pocket: three tens, a five, and four bucks. Tearing them in half I gave him one part, said, "After tonight you get the rest, go on a week's drunk if you want. But for the next couple of hours you're working for me, and don't forget it."

Dewey fingered the torn money. "Marty, why the green salad?"

"A reminder that if you make a mistake I won't be around to give you the rest of the lettuce," I said, pocketing the torn bills. "Your job is simple: I don't want you to leave the desk—not for a second, even if the Grover is on fire. You're being paid to stay by your phone. And to take good care of this." I placed the letter addressed to Bill in Dewey's lap. "Don't let anybody get ahold of that letter, even see it—till later. Understand?"

Dewey nodded.

I gave him a slip of paper with Lande's store phone on it. "And keep this handy, too. All right, here's the deal. Starting at ten o'clock you call this number every fifteen minutes. No matter if the desk is busy or not, every fifteen minutes you call. I'll answer and say, 'Lawson is a fag.' That's all. You don't answer anything except one word, 'Okay, Marty.' But if ..."

"That's two words."

"All right! Goddamnit, Dewey, you just answer, 'Okay, Marty.' Not another sound. Now, when you ring and there isn't any answer, or if somebody else answers, says, 'Hello?' says anything but 'Lawson is a fag,' you hang up—and call Bill Ash fast at the number on the envelope. That's the police station. Tell him—or whoever answers at the precinct—that you want a cop damn fast. If Ash answers tell him you have something important and he must come and get it—at once. You only give this letter to Ash, and ask to see his badge, or to a uniformed cop. Got it?"

Dewey swallowed, his eyes watered, and he touched the envelope like it was hot. "Marty, you in something ... something ... real bad?"

"This is all the way for me, Dewey. That's why I want you to stay off the wine and on the ball. Remember, if anybody answers with anything but our passwords, don't you say a single word, just slam the receiver down and call the police. And for Christ's sake, be sure you're dialing the right number, the one on the slip. Now, tell me what I told you."

Dewey stuttered through it and we went over it again. Then I told him, "Good. Finish the pint—you'll need that. Stay at the desk, and remember—start calling at ten sharp. Even if you have to go to the john—stay at the desk!"

Dewey stood up, put Bill's letter in his back pocket, Lande's phone number in his shirt pocket. He asked, "Marty, what are you in? Will I ...?"

"You'll be a lousy hero. One more thing, don't blab about this to Kenny, Barbara—nobody."

"Listen, Marty, you know how I am—maybe I won't be able to ..."

He was shaking a little and I slapped him on the back. "Just do what I told you and everything will be okay. Hell, we're pals, you're the only one I can trust. Get going. Remember, you start phoning at ten sharp—about an hour and a half from now. 'Lawson is a fag.' If anybody says anything else, even if you *think* it's me, hang up and call the cops. Get going."

When he left I put the carbon of the letter in an envelope, addressed it to the kid in the hospital, then put the rest of the torn money in another envelope addressed to Dewey. I dug up a couple of stamps, locked my door, and dropped the letters in the mail chute off the lobby. I took the self-service elevator to the eighth floor, opened the linen-closet window, stepped out on the adjoining fire escape—the weight of the .45 at my ankle making me clumsy.

I went up and over the roof, down into the alley, moving carefully. After last night they'd be wondering how I got out of the Grover. Dropping into the alley as softly as my two-hundred-odd pounds would allow, I stood very still in the darkness.

I had company—somebody in front of me was breathing heavily.

I stood there for a long moment, fingering the gun in my pocket, retasting the sea food, trying not to belch.

Whoever was sharing the alley with me was making a

lot of noise with his breathing. I waited, but my buddy was playing it cool. I got my flash out, knelt and placed it on the cement alleyway, pointing it in the general direction of the breathing.

I got my gun out and leaning way over to the right, I reached out with my left foot, pressed the button. I spotlighted an old bum huddled in one corner. I grinned as he blinked his bleary eyes to get me in focus.

I pocketed the gun and picking up my flash I started toward him. He said, "Put that light out, you big sonofabitch."

"They making you winos braver these days?" I asked.

I was on top of him and he sort of grinned and his teeth were too good for a wino and his eyes were too bright—he wasn't drunk—he was on junk. He was sitting with both hands on the cement and he raised himself off the floor a few inches as his legs struck out, scissored around mine.

I fell on top of him, kicking, swinging with my flash … and thought I heard the swish of a sap behind me before my head exploded in a burning white flame.

Six

I came to on my side, part of my head and neck feeling big as a ton—a numb ton. There was light near me and after blinking a few times, I managed to sit up and look around. The wino decoy was lying a couple of feet from me, blood streaming from his head: I must have followed through with my swing before I conked out.

Turning made my head spin, but I finally faced the light. The face above the small flashlight was Hilly Smith's, all the sharp, overneat features. His eyes were as cold and impersonal as dry ice. For a moment I couldn't see any hands, then I realized he was wearing dark gloves. He must have been holding my Police Special in his right hand—it seemed suspended in the dim light—the business end pointing at me.

I belched and my head hurt. But I moved my legs a little. Bob wasn't any ball of fire; he hadn't found the .45.

We stared at each other for a while. I'd seen him once or twice over the years, but never this close. He was a handsome punk, tall and lean, with wide sloping shoulders. His face was hard and without an ounce of fat, or maybe it was the shadows that made him look so hard.

I put my elbows on the cement ground and relaxed, wondering what the next move was. I'd walked into a trap, but it didn't make any difference to me. Dewey would call Bill at ten when I didn't answer. Even if the wine got to Dewey, Lawrence would have the carbon copy of the letter in the morning and then they'd pick up Bochio, maybe Smith. All I had to do was see to it I didn't leave the alley alive. And if Bob made a mistake, I'd like to knock him off. Sort of a going-away present to somebody ... maybe myself. A kind of ...

He said, "What's ya story, ya bastid?" There was something wrong with his lips, like they were too big for his mouth—they didn't stop at his face, went inside his mouth. Or maybe that was the shadows too.

"I was going to tell it to you—in Willie's shop. But this is just as good a spot." My voice sounded strong in the stillness.

"Figured that. But didn't want to knock ya off in the store, too much explaining."

"What explaining?" I said, mocking him. "You could do me like you did Cocky, knock me off in the freezer, then dump the body any time you felt like it. Bochio must have thought he was real clever; shoots him, then goes down to Miami and establishes his alibi. Couple of weeks later you dump the body in the Bronx, it lays in the heat all day and no medical examiner can say it was frozen, that Anderson *wasn't* shot the night before. That's old stuff—he wasn't so smart."

"A knife in the back is old—but it still works."

The "bum" near me groaned and then was silent again.

Bob stared at him for a moment, then turned to me, asked, "What was ya doing, giving a public lecture?" He moved fast, jumped to my side and kicked me before I knew what was happening. As I doubled up he split the side of my face with my own gun.

I didn't black out, but for a long time I couldn't move, could hardly breathe. Blood was flowing into my shirt collar, down my side like syrupy sweat. I began to doubt Bob was going to make a mistake.... Then I had a frightening thought: Maybe he wasn't going to kill me, only work me over to scare me off?

I waited till I could sit up again, sure I could move my legs. My only play was a corny one; the decoy had used it on me.

Smith said, "I know all about ya, big hero copper now a two-bit lush, a lousy hotel dick. Who ya working for on this?"

When I opened my mouth, blood ran in and damn near choked me.

"What ya trying to do, make a name for yourself, get back on the force?"

"I want in," I said, and it sounded like I was talking through a mouthful of mud.

"In—a shakedown?" He laughed, but no sound came out.

I tried to nod and my head seemed to be coming off. "Killing me won't do no good," I said, and my voice came back strong and clear the more I talked. "I sent a letter to myself care of general delivery; with a cop as the return address. If I don't call for it ... tomorrow ... it goes back, will be opened.... You and Bochio will fry." It wasn't much of a story, but it would do.

"Ya think ya're playing with kids, ya bastid!"

"No, I think it's time to separate the men from the boys, Bob."

He didn't say anything for a moment, those ice-eyes watching me. I was in a sudden panic he might walk away, leave me. I said, "I never would have got onto this if you had learned to talk straight. You talk like a backward ..."

He kicked me in the ear. For a second my head seemed to balloon up, then everything became clear again. "Every kick only jacks up the price. You and Bochio made a lot of mistakes by shooting Cocky in the freezer—don't make no more. Why did Bochio have to become a hood again after all these years? Start messing around with a perfect crime, no less?"

The "decoy" groaned again and Bob clouted him with the gun, knocking him into silence.

He said to me, "I told ya, no lectures!"

I was getting weaker, my whole shirt wet with blood. I lowered my voice as if I was passing out, said, "Everything is in ... the ... letter, Bochio probably never even knew Lande ...was ... a ... relative. Or maybe Willie never knew. Then Bochio gets this ... this ... yen to kill Cocky. Maybe saw this freeze deal in a movie ... or something. Looks around for a butcher, a freezer, and there's ... one ... right in the family. All in the ... the ... letter."

"Ya lousy chiseling bastid, whatcha want?"

"Ten grand," I whispered.

Bob bent over me a little. "Whatcha say?"

"Ten grand." I wanted to smile. Bob Smith the syndicate cop—a dumb punk.

He was almost stepping over my legs as he repeated, "Ten grand?"

1 muttered, "If ... I ... die, you're done."

"Ya think we're dumb enough to pay off, so ya'll keep shaking us down!"

I waved my hand. "Sure I will ... but small stuff. I ... I know when not to ... overplay my hand." I ended this in a mumble of double talk.

"What? Talk louder."

I gasped out something neither of us could hear and inched my right leg out. Even if I didn't make it he'd shoot me dead.

"Ya're a muscleman—ya know I can do things that will, make ya talk, beg for the finisher!"

"The letter ... remember that," I said loud enough for him to hear. "Get me to a doc before ... I die."

He hesitated and I mumbled, "I'm ... dying!" and stiffened like a ham actor—getting my right leg way out.

Bob bent lower. "Hey! Ya get the dough! Hey!" he repeated like an idiot. Blood was forming in my mouth and I gargled with a little of it, sounded like a death rattle.

He stood up and I thought I'd overdone it. But he pulled out a fistful of money, bent down and waved it in my face. "Here, ya get the dough! Ya hear? Ya get ..."

I put everything I had into swinging my right leg—with the .45 strapped against it—into a long arc as Bob tried to straighten up. There was the blast of my own gun—in his hand—that seemed to go off in my eyes as my leg clouted him on the side of his face.

Smith fell over sideways as I tried to sit up in the blast that blinded me. After the flash of gunpowder, the darkness was awful dark and it took me a long time to see. But it didn't take any time to feel the pain in my shoulder where he'd shot me. I could move my left arm so it wasn't too bad, but it took me a lot of years before I was able to stand. On my feet I felt much better.

I picked up Hilly's flash and looked at the "bum." His head and face were all blood, but he was alive—the blood was bubbling at his lips. I straightened up. Bending down hadn't done me any good. I was dripping blood so badly it was really sloshing around in my shoes.

Blood never worried me and I had things to do. I took a deep breath, like a weightlifter, and dragged Bob over to a corner of the alley, set him up where he would be a dead duck in my private shooting gallery. The effort about kayoed me and I had to lean against the wall myself for a bunch of seconds. It was funny, the way I could move now, wasn't scared when I wasn't doing my own killing.

Bob started to move and I kicked his head against the wall, careful not to kill him ... ruin my angle in this mess. I put the flash down so it covered us and frisked him. He had a gun on his hip and another up his sleeve. The sleeve job would be a lousy small-caliber deal, meaning only a lucky shot or a brace of slugs would do me in. I didn't touch the sleeve rod—that had to be it. The money he'd offered me was laying in his lap and for some stupid reason I picked up a few of the hundred-dollar bills, then picked up the flash with my left hand. My left was too bloody and the flash slipped out, and broke on the cement.

I stood up in the darkness, trying to steady myself, cursing my stupidity. Both Bob and I would need light. I bent over Bob, ripped off part of his coat, stumbled over to the bum and ripped off his coat and pants. I made a pile of the clothing, dropped the money on top of it. Then I made a small pile of a few crumpled bills twisted together, lit them with my lighter. I put Bob's gun and my Police Special near him where he could see them, but out of his reach. I wiped my hands and put the .45 in my pocket. The burning bills died out and I leaned against the wall, shut my eyes till my head cleared ... and waited.

After what seemed hours and had to be seconds, I heard Bob moan, then sit up. I got my lighter out and lit the bills atop the clothing.

Bob stared at me through bloody eyes, one side of his face puffed and out of shape. He rubbed his wrist against his thigh and probably smiled behind the blood, thinking I'd overlooked the gun there. I don't know why but suddenly, for the first time in my life, the sight of blood, beaten skin, made me a little sick.

Swaying in front of him, right hand on the .45 straining my pocket, the stinking fire throwing crazy shadows all around us, I said, "At last I got me a real big hood. The top syndicate cop. You thought you were outside the law, outside of me, had your own law. Even took care of the punks who robbed Willie. Were you scared they might have seen Cocky's corpse in the freezer? But for once I ..."

"The money!" Bob gasped. It sounded like his jaw was busted. "Ya're ... in!"

"In what? You dumb clown, I don't want no money. I'm going to work you over, beat your brains out, leave you crippled for life ... if you live." I wasn't hearing my own words. I was thinking beating a punk no longer seemed important or necessary to me.

The fire was dying and I said, "I'm going to leave you so you'll never hurt another ..."

Bob really was good—a snap of the wrist I might never have noticed if I didn't know about the gun, and one of these runty European automatics was in his right hand. Maybe it was the weird light from the fire, but the gun seemed to spark like a toy cap pistol. All I felt was two sharp quick stabs in my gut.

Smith actually hissed as he said, "Bastid copper! Dumb bastid copper!" as I came toward him. Two more of those toy sparks and I knew I was hit in the gut again. Now the pain came, deep and burning.

I was almost on top of him when he let me have the last two. It didn't seem possible but I only felt one stab—the jerk missed with the other shot.

The dizziness and pain were mounting fast, but I could still handle my gun ... although I knew I was swaying like the shadows from the last of the fire, and smoke seemed to fog my eyes as I said, "All right, that's me—a *copper!*" and let him have the .45 from my coat pocket.

Part of his head bounced against the wall as the boom of the .45 covered me with thunder—thunder that had nothing to do with me starting to fall backward.

Outside of Bridgehampton out on Long Island there's a wonderful lonely beach called Sagaponack, an Indian name. It's miles of clean sand and high dunes and sometimes thundering waves. It's the finest beach I know for surf casting, and we'd usually get the idea around nine or ten at night, hop into somebody's heap and be out there by midnight, fish till morning. The pounding waves send up a salt spray that fills the air, and when the sun starts to come up, this haze turns a faint pink, shot through with a hundred rainbows. Sometimes, when I was out there alone, it all seemed out of this world, really out.

When I opened my eyes I saw this pink fog moving gently around me and when I could think I thought, If there is such a thing as Heaven or Hell I'm sunk, played my cards wrong all down the line. Or am I back on the beach? And how did I get here?

I didn't try to move, just stared at the pink air. Then I

got it figured—I was still in the alley seeing daylight through the blood on my face. But I should be a corpse ... no man lives through the night with five slugs in his belly, a busted head and a ...

The pink faded to a mild yellow and then after a long time became a clean hard white. I kept working my eyes and damn if I wasn't in a hospital room!

There couldn't be any doubt. Although I couldn't seem to move my eyes much, I saw the white metal stingy table and chair you find only in a hospital. I tried moving, but even turning my head was such a big deal I gave it up. Something red and white flashed before my eyes. I got the frightened face of a red-headed nurse into focus, heard her call, "Dr. Moorepark! Dr. Moorepark—he's regained consciousness!"

The redhead disappeared and there wasn't a single sound after that as I stared at the white table. I'd sure slopped up things. Then I heard voices, felt something on my skin and finally a pinprick that seemed a mile away. I could almost feel real strength, hot and firm, rushing through me. A joker who looked like a movie doctor—the quiet puss with the brushed gray hair and terribly tired eyes—shoved his big head into view, asked, "Mr. Bond, can you hear me?" The voice was deep and sure.

He was so near I could hear the sloshing sound his moving lips made. "Sure, I can hear you. Why ain't I dead? What went wrong?"

The face came even nearer, the lips seemed on top of my eyes. I could see all his fillings. "Mr. Bond, can you hear me?"

"Said I could. Get out of my face."

The thin wet lips moved again. "We have very little time, Mr. Bond, and you're not making any sound. If you hear me, will you please blink your eyes."

What was wrong with my mouth? I could hear my own voice—this joker must be deaf. I blinked.

"Mr. Bond, we've given you a ... You will sleep shortly so I must be frank with you. You were—and are—badly hurt. It's only a surgical miracle you are alive at all. I am telling you this because you are strong and have a good chance of living—if you fight for it." The lips moved faster as the voice took on a selling tone. "I know you want to live because you are the biggest name in the news these last few days, a national hero! You have a big future before you, a ..."

I shut my eyes. There was more talk I didn't listen to, something about Flo waiting for me.... Then a new voice said, "Marty, please look at me."

I opened my eyes to see Art Dupre, the rugged earnest face before me. He had that bursting-with-good-news look in his eyes as he said, "Marty, you old iron man! I happened to be ... Marty, when they brought you in all shot open, I had a sample made—you haven't got cancer!"

Art took a breath, almost shouted in my face, "Marty, do you understand, your tumor is *not* malignant! Truth is it's not even a tumor but a kind of pocket in the intestines in which food gets caught and decays and ... Hell, Marty, you get it, you were all wrong about cancer! All you have to do is work with us and in a few weeks you'll be up and around, good as new. Marty old man, you have to ..."

I closed my eyes, the lids were starting to weigh a ton.

"Marty, tell me you've heard me, that you know you haven't cancer?"

I blinked as fast as I could, saw Art's lean puss run over with relief. Then I kept my eyes closed and after a while I was back in the pink haze, the voice lost in the distance.

For a split second I wanted to work out signals with my eyes, tell Art. But it was too tiring and complicated and it didn't matter. Not even cancer or being free of cancer mattered.

How could I ever explain to Art—or why should I?—that I had seen Marty Bond a little too clearly these last few days, that I didn't want to live. Marty the bully-boy should never have been born, never have ...

The pink mist became a deeper red. The sun must be coming out stronger, but the air and the sand were damp and cold. Something jerked at the rod real sharp, then another big jerk. I dropped my beach blanket as I stood up, grabbed the rod. I sure had a fighter hooked, I could barely hold the rod. I said, "Watch me reel this baby in. Got something big, maybe a baby tuna or a hell of a blue. Will you look at the battle the slimy fool is giving me—damn near snapping the rod."

"His pulse is getting weaker. Mr. Bond! Mr. Bond!"

The rod was straining so I couldn't turn to see who was talking. The fish never slacked up. Instead it seemed to grow stronger, hitting the line again and again with a steady pull. It was a hell of a fish. My arms began to ache, the rod was slipping out of my hands. It was a regular damn whale. I don't know how the line held, but the jerking was too much for me to haul in, or even hold on to.

The rod began to shake and I made one last effort to hold it....

Then I let go.

THE END

ED LACY BIBLIOGRAPHY
(1911-1968)

Walk Hard—Talk Loud
(1940 as by Len Zinberg)

What D'ya Know for Sure
(1947 as by Len Zinberg;
revised as Strange
Desires, 1949)

Hold With the Hares
(1948 as by Len Zinberg)

The Woman Aroused
(1951)

Sin in Their Blood (1952;
published in UK as Death
in Passing, 1959)

Strip for Violence (1953)

Enter Without Desire
(1954)

Go for the Body (1954)

Exit 13 (1954; as by Steve
April)

The Best That Ever Did It
(1955; reprinted in pb as
Visa to Death, 1956)

The Men from the Boys
(1956)

Lead with Your Left
(1957)***

Room to Swing (1957)*

Breathe No More, My
Lady (1958)

Shakedown for Murder
(1958)

Be Careful How You Live
(1958)

Blonde Bait (1959)

The Big Fix (1960)

A Deadly Affair (1960)

Bugged for Murder (1961)

The Freeloaders (1961)

South Pacific Affair (1961)

The Sex Castle (1963;
reprinted as Shoot It
Again,1969)

Two Hot to Handle (1963;
two novellas: The Coin of
Adventure and Murder in
Paradise)

Moment of Untruth
(1964)*

Harlem Underground
(1965)**

Pity the Honest (1965)

The Hotel Dwellers (1966)

Double Trouble (1967)***

In Black & Whitey
(1967)**

The Napalm Bugle (1968)

The Big Bust (1969)

*Toussaint M. Moore series
**Lee Hayes series
*** Dave Wintino series

Ed Lacy was born Leonard "Len" S. Zinberg in New York City on August 25, 1911. During the late 1920s, he attended the College of the City of New York, then wandered the U.S. in the next decade working odd jobs. Returning to New York in the early 40s, he married Esther, and except for a stint in the army in WWII, lived with his wife and daughter in New York City on the fringes of Harlem the rest of his life. A huge fight fan, Zinberg's first published novel in 1940 was a boxing story, and became a Broadway play. He went on to create "the first credible African-American PI," Touie Moore, in *Room to Swing*, which won the Edgar for Best Novel in 1958. Overall, Zinberg published 29 novels and over 90 short stories before his death by heart attack on January 7, 1968.

Black Gat Books

Black Gat Books is a new line of mass market paperbacks introduced in 2015 by Stark House Press. New titles appear every three months, featuring the best in crime fiction reprints. Each book is sized to 4.25" x 7", just like they used to be. Collect them all!

1 Haven for the Damned
by Harry Whittington
978-1-933586-75-5, $9.99

2 Eddie's World
by Charlie Stella
978-1-933586-76-2, $9.99

3 Stranger at Home
by Leigh Brackett writing as
George Sanders
978-1-933586-78-6, $9.99

4 The Persian Cat
by John Flagg
978-1933586-90-8, $9.99

5 Only the Wicked
by Gary Phillips
978-1-933586-93-9, $9.99

6 Felony Tank
by Malcolm Braly
978-1-933586-91-5, $9.99

7 The Girl on the Bestseller List
by Vin Packer
978-1-933586-98-4, $9.99

8 She Got What She Wanted
by Orrie Hitt
978-1-944520-04-5, $9.99

9 The Woman on the Roof
by Helen Nielsen
978-1-944520-13-7, $9.99

10 Angel's Flight
by Lou Cameron
978-1-944520-18-2, $9.99

11 The Affair of Lady
Westcott's Lost Ruby /
The Case of the Unseen Assassin
by Gary Lovisi
978-1-944520-22-9, $9.99

12 The Last Notch
by Arnold Hano
978-1-944520-31-1, $9.99

13 Never Say No to a Killer
by Clifton Adams
978-1-944520-36-6, $9.99

Stark House Press

1315 H Street, Eureka, CA 95501 707-498-3135
griffinskye3@sbcglobal.net www.starkhousepress.com

Available from your local bookstore or direct from the publisher.

Made in the USA
Las Vegas, NV
23 December 2023